AILUROS

AILUROS

BY MATT DOYLE

ISBN: 978-1-7368183-7-4 (Paperback)
ISBN: 978-1-7368183-8-1 (Hardcover)

Library of Congress Control Number: 2021945104

Any references to historical events, real people, or real places are used fictitiously. Names, characters, and places are products of the author's imagination.

Book design by Allison Chernutan.

Printed in the United States of America.

First printing edition 2021.

emily@fracturedmirrorpublishing.com
Fractured Mirror Publishing
Knoxville, Tennessee

www.fracturedmirrorpublishing.com

For those whose paths are sometimes cracked, and the ones that just seek wonder.

For the ones who are not stopping long but are always staying longer.

For those forgotten, and the ones passed by.

For the ones still fighting as though they'll die.

For those who simply need a lift, and the ones that are euphoric too.

For the ones that should not, cannot, will, and must, my friends, this one is for you.

FILE INTRODUCTION

The following report represents a summary of the incident involving the abandoned microgravity holiday destination, Ailuros Unit Twenty-Three, and the crew of the Salvagers Guild Three ship, The Orca. The report is comprised primarily of the official transcripts of both the aforementioned events on board the unit and my interview with Guild Director, Sarah Walker. The final entry consists of my summarizing thoughts on the case. As is often the case in investigations such as this, in the end, Ailuror itself is as much the key to understanding the events as the people involved are. Circumstances as well as personal choices are important, after all. Please note, as per standard practises, transcriber names have been redacted.

Case Reference: 43750919081521120414200801205
Additional Materials Reference: 4375030112120504080913022120009
Investigative Officer: Mark Tyler
UNID Staff Number: 121519202008050609070820

[1] Dear Josh. I'm sorry. It feels strange saying that now. There's a part of me that feels like I shouldn't apologize at all, all things considered. But there it is. I drugged your tea. I know you opted out of Neg-Vacs, and on medical advice at that, but I was desperate. The thing is, I saw you. With him. And no matter how much I tried to hint at knowing it, you just wouldn't open up. I needed you to be willing to open up unprompted. Or that's what I thought at the time. After seeing what I did, I skipped my own Neg-Vac. I didn't want it all suppressed. I wanted to feel the full force of it. But it didn't happen. You didn't bite. So, I took my Neg-Vac and used it to drug your tea, then put you in my Alleviation Sim. Yes, I'm aware that there are dangers with that; the mix is custom built for each person, based on their physiology. The way the whole system works is, I guess. That would be why 'Ailuros' came up as 'Ailuror' in the introduction. The AI was trying to reconcile words based on my brain, not yours. I wouldn't be surprised if that isn't the only one it gets wrong.

Like I said, I was desperate. I suppose that doesn't really excuse it though, does it? I essentially risked your life because I allowed myself to feel jealous. And angry. The worst thing is, that's not even where it ends. After I got back on the Neg-Vac, I stole this report—technically it was addressed to me but being about you makes it yours—and took it to a friend of mine that works freelance in Waking Dream Analysis. I won't give you their name, but I will say that they've been used by a couple of companies before now when crime has been suspected. Basically, they know what they're doing. They reviewed your Alleviation Sim. You'll recognize their notes because they'll be shown <like this>. The rest of the stuff you'll read is mine. So, you know what? I do owe you an apology. I'm sorry. For screwing up and nearly killing you, and for showing your private data to someone else. But I needed to know. I needed to know if any part of you was sorry, too, or if there's any chance that we can salvage something from this. Anyway. Read on. I'm writing in order as I read, so I don't know what I'll find.

[2] I recognized this wording straight away. You said the same thing about the Neg-Vac/Alleviation Sim system during our first date. I always thought you just didn't like the way the Government controls how we experience 'recognized negative emotions.' Even with the evidence that the system works—violent crime is down 86% after all—some push back is natural. Still though, 'a trial.' Maybe you were always a little scared about what would come out if someone put you in a Sim.

FILE NAME: EXPLORATORY INTERVIEW (I)
FILE REFERENCE: 4375122103259127003361002959 40
TRANSCRIBED BY: ███ ██

MARK TYLER: My[1] name is Mark Tyler, acting legal representative for the UNID in the case of Ailuros Unit Twenty-Three. My interview subject today is Sarah Walker, current Director of Salvagers Guild Three. Sarah, do you give consent for the recording, both audio and video, of our conversation?

SARAH WALKER: I do.

MARK TYLER: And do you consent to the verbatim transcription of this conversation to be provided to the necessary legal bodies including, where appropriate, my own notes and assessment?

SARAH WALKER: I do.

MARK TYLER: Finally, do you consent to the use of standard UNID monitors, designed with the intent to indicate, but not legally confirm, potential falsehoods in statements made by yourself.

SARAH WALKER: I do.

MARK TYLER: Okay, good. Thank you. A copy of all evidence within the case file will, of course, be provided to you upon compilation. Now, are you fine with me calling you Sarah, or would you prefer Miss Walker?

SARAH WALKER: Sarah is fine.

MARK TYLER: You seem very defensive, Sarah.

SARAH WALKER: What do you expect? This is for all intents and purposes the first stages of a trial,[2] isn't it?

MARK TYLER: To an extent. As such though, you should be well aware that the more information you can provide, the better. Neither I nor the UNID are your enemies, Sarah. However, in the spirit of honesty, I will say this. This is not a case of whether charges can be raised, but rather, *which* charges can be raised. And against whom. The events aboard

[3] It isn't how I expected it to go either. I'll be honest, now that I'm thinking clearly again, doing this feels dirty. Then, I remember why I'm doing it. Even with the medication suppression, the pain is still there. I guess that makes it one of those 'high stress anomalies' the guides talk about, doesn't it? It doesn't make it easier, just more justifiable. At least to me.

[4] <An indication that the subject's unconscious mind is aware that something has happened and is trying to figure out the cause.>
The fact is, no matter what else is in play here, you made a choice to sleep with him. So, it's you Josh. You are to blame, even if not entirely.

[5] <It is too soon to be certain, but this opening section seems to be indicative of an attempt at self-study. It is clear that there will be multiple characters in the Sim. Each will be representative of a part of the subject, whether it be a personality trait, or simply the embodiment of an event. Mark and Sarah discussing the events is an attempt to bring it all together into a cohesive whole.>

I read up a little on this way back when I was put in the Neg-Vac system. Supressing negative emotions and traits usually leads to everything being condensed in the Sim. You relive a direct event or something easily linkable, and it's always from your own point of view. That yours isn't here is part of the reason for you being medically cleared to avoid the injections. To be clear, I'm not saying you're broken. I'm saying you're complicated. So many things affect you. And giving you my Neg-Vac probably made that worse.

Ailuros Unit Twenty Three have ramifications, some of them far reaching, and not just for Salvagers Guild Three.

SARAH WALKER: [Sighs] I understand that. This isn't exactly how I expected things to go, you know?[3]

MARK TYLER: [Nods] I can imagine. Nevertheless, we do need to get to the bottom of what exactly happened.

SARAH WALKER: And who's to blame?[4]

MARK TYLER: That too. Now, the way this works is we're going to review the relevant files in order. As we do so, I will be asking you questions regarding different points. You are free to ask any questions you wish to, of course, and if I can answer them, I will.[5] Each conversation we have will be stored as a separate file for the purposes of the overall case file, but as the recording itself is continuous,there won't be a need to repeat consent.

SARAH WALKER: Sounds fine to me. I run internal reviews the same way.

MARK TYLER: Glad to hear it. Well then. We'll begin with some background files.

[6] <Reading ahead slightly, I noted that the subject has placed themselves and their partner in the lead roles. While not the first to appear in the Sim, they are the first to appear in the 'events' the Sim is covering. When you consider the fractured nature of the scenario, this demonstrates that he is aware that the negative emotions he is dealing with relates directly to both him and his partner.>

This is good. It means we're dealing with the right stuff. If this had gone another way, it would be a waste. That sounds bad, actually. I mean a waste in terms of what I want to achieve. Which is selfish. Which is a recognized negative emotion. I guess I'm still in that run on you get when you come off then go back on the Neg-Vacs.

[7] The 'throwback' mentioned here is, in reality, your habit of focusing on the past. You always talked about relationships that failed. And you were also sad when you did. It hurt knowing that you had as much time, if not more, for past lovers as you did for me. I buried my feelings about it because it was all a part of you. Maybe that was my mistake. If I'd spoken to you about it, perhaps this could have prevented. Or maybe you would have kept it all in more and it would have been worse? Who knew being a wailing wall could hurt so much, eh? Still. I wonder if what I've done will be something you speak about with your next lover.

[8] This was random but I did recognize the title. It's one of your favourites. The study of the secret communications between an online political activist and the UK PM, and the cryptography used to crack their systems. You're a little prone to paranoia, I think, especially when it comes to the Government. You were obsessed with the idea that there was something more nefarious going on and that you needed to hide things from the powers that be. At least on your bad days. You know, before I knew that it was something that hurt you, I used to like how you had hidden codes in your record keeping and social media posts. It was a cute quirk. Or that's what I thought. I grew to appreciate how consuming paranoia can be through living with you. You helped me grow a little like that. It seemed unfair really that all I could do was watch and listen, rather than help you grow past it.

[9] <Deities often appear in these Sims as having a direct link to judgement. It's symptomatic of how much religion has been used to justify judgement over the years. The use of a deity as part of the place that the characters are aiming to reach, and the earlier mention of 'a trial' confirms this, which would make the Ailuros unit somewhere where the subject's 'sins' will be played out and laid bare. I am unfamiliar with the Goddess' lore though, so cannot confirm if the name holds any relevance beyond being known to the subject.>

The name here is actually slightly wrong. Ailuros was the Greek name for the Egyptian Goddess, Bast. Her Greek equivalent would be Artemis, I think. It is interesting though. Bast was a cat-headed deity, and I refer to you as 'Puss-Puss' in the Sim. That she was a Goddess of protection and cats might mean you were hoping for divine intervention?

Josh Byrne[6] floated gently in the middle of The Wanderer's rec room. He'd insisted on it being set up to mimic a twenty-first century London living room when he first moved into the ship. There was just something about that aesthetic that he loved. Even the way the room lights were humming had a charm to it.

But then, he'd always been a retro-tech throwback.[7] Some things were unavoidable of course, such as the mandated Skin Suits. Designed to allow people to wear projections of whatever clothing they wanted, they certainly had advantages. Projection routines were far cheaper to buy than real clothing, for example, which all but eliminated certain types of bullying.

Plus, Alex got that vintage "little black dress projection" that they both loved, albeit for slightly different reasons.

Josh flipped a page on his well-worn copy of KeepTalking//PieceByPiece's *The Toby Garvin Regime: Lost Interviews with the Prime Minister*,[8] and took in the scent of the paper. He sighed.

"Hey Puss-Puss. Found your catnip again?"

Josh smiled and glanced up at the video screen on the wall. "Still far better than the synthesized scent the eBooks use."

Alex Holden chuckled, and continued, "You'll never guess what I found on the scanner."

Josh flipped another page. "A derelict?"

Alex tutted and stuck their tongue out. "You know, it's no fun if you don't play along. I mean, you could have said anything. A new planet. Alien life. A decent off-world coffee."

"Okay, okay," Josh laughed. "So, what have we found?"

"You ever hear of Ailuros?"

"Microgravity Ibiza, right? The holiday station named after the Greek goddess of dance and beauty. [9]"

"Amongst other things. Anyway, two and a half years ago, they ejected one of their holiday units. We just happen to have found it."

Josh stopped reading and frowned. "That's potentially a pretty big haul. We should get onto the guild."

"Oh, I already called it in," Alex replied, relaxing their arms behind their

[10] For what it's worth, I blushed at that. I always did appreciate it when you complimented me. The same applied to the little black dress comment. And by the way, you were only partially right on us liking it for different reasons. Yes, it does make me feel more comfortable on female-leaning days, and it is more of a sex thing for you. I do enjoy the physical side too though. Between the way the projection makes it hang and how much you enjoy it, how could I not feel sexy? This helps, actually. Remembering the ways we're good for each other reminds me why I want to save what we have. I just hope you see it the same way when you see what I've done.

head and smiling widely. "We're on our way to see Sarah right now. ETA three hours."

"In that case," Josh replied, pressing a bookmark against his page, "I'll grab the coffee. A decent off-world one, right?"

"Best make mine a water for now; I'm due a treadmill session," Alex replied, then added, in a low purr, "I trust that means you'll be with me shortly?"

Josh blushed and made no attempt to hide it. "Best view out there.[10] See you in five."

The speaker clicked off, and Josh folded a magnetized band around the book. He looked over at the bookshelf, took aim, and pushed the book, letting it float freely. He grabbed one of the floor bars and pulled himself forward, using the microgravity to travel alongside the old paperback.

The book slid gently into place between two others, making a satisfying click as the band was drawn against the magnetic strip at the back of the shelf. Josh threw his arms up in celebration, grabbed the doorway, and slipped into the hall.

[11] <Though seemingly a throwaway comment, this is an important one. Sarah dealing with multiple issues is indicative of there being multiple things that the subject needs to let out. This is not necessarily multiple different events to work through, but more likely a complicated mix of emotions relating to one thing. The use of 'again' though means this probably isn't the first time this has happened. It should be noted that this doesn't confirm the event itself has happened multiple times, but rather may simply reference the introspection.>

[12] He found you first. But you were with me. You knew that acting on what you still felt for him was wrong though. You must have. If you didn't then we've both lost this fight already.

[13] <Negligent arsehole is self-judgemental. It may be that the subject feels like they could have prevented what happened from happening if they'd been more careful.>

Interloper is probably how he viewed me given how soon after you split we got together. Well, sort of. You were very on-again, off-again until you took that final step. As to negligence though, that would be an understatement really. You don't accidentally sleep with someone.

[14] <Rules of acquisition and the concept of the case not being straightforward can be taken as the interaction between the subject's current relationship and the complexities of his emotions relating to the event that he is dealing with here.>

Internally, I suppose it isn't. I've seen people that I thought were hot, and I've met exes that I had good times with, so I get it on some level. We complicate things as a species, and sometimes, working out what we're feeling is hard. I can forgive you for wavering. Please understand that. Mistakes happen. You're right though. It's not straight forward. It never is. In a way, it'd be easier if I could look at this and say, 'you knew what you were doing, and just didn't care.' To come to that conclusion would be unfair though. That the scenario is manifesting the way it is means you did care. That makes it harder. That I care, even more so.

Sarah Walker, director of Salvagers Guild Three, rubbed her eyes and stared at the comms hub. It was making a loud beep and flashing up a message confirming that she had an incoming call.

Again.[11]

She grunted and hit the 'accept' button. "This is Sarah. What's the problem now?"

"Nice." It was Lucy Foster, clearly sat at the bridge of her ship, Foster's Hope. Her projected auburn hair hung scruffily at her shoulders, moving gently as she intermittently tensed. She looked pissed off. "We just had a claim denied. Care to explain that?"

"The automated response should confirm the reason for any denial of—"

"You're fucking right it does," Lucy cut in. "It says The Wanderer got the salvage. An hour after our scanners picked up the derelict."

Sarah sighed. "Hang on. Let me check this."

She swiped the call screen to the side and pulled a list of recent acquirements, filtering out all ships but The Wanderer and Foster's Hope. "It says here that you only put the claim in half an hour ago?"

"We were busy," Lucy grunted, throwing her arms up in disbelief.

Sarah dropped her elbow onto the desk and leaned forward, rubbing her temple. "Both you and Aaron know the rules, Lucy. If Alex and Josh got their claim in first, it doesn't technically matter whether you found it first."[12]

Lucy's eyes narrowed and her lips pulled back into a sneer. "Okay then, what about etiquette? Or the fact that you're allowing a salvage to pass from a team with no blemishes to one comprised of an interloper and a negligent arsehole?"[13]

Sarah listened to Lucy rant and absently called up the claims, curious as to what would cause this level of hostility. When she saw the registered name of the derelict, she frowned. "Wait. This is…okay, look. The rules of acquisition are unbendable. This isn't a straight-forward case though.[14] The Wanderer should be docking within the next hour and a half. I need to check a few things, then I'll decide what to do."

"Fine," Lucy snapped. "We're heading in too."

"Do *not* try to start any trouble with Alex and Josh. Do you understand?"

“Whatever. “

Sarah fixed Lucy's image with a glare, pushing her authority into her eyes. “I mean it, Lucy.”

Lucy rolled her eyes. “Fine. You have my word that I will not do anything to Alex Holden or Josh Byrne.”

“Good.”

[15] Is this resentment for not being able to play the field a little? When you see beautiful people but know you shouldn't act on impulse? My friend said it's possible. That's the thing with analysis from a personal viewpoint; I'll pick up somethings because I know you, and they'll pick up others because they studied for this.

<It should be noted that, to a degree, this is still guesswork. Informed guesswork, but still guesswork.>

[16] That's a significant word. You left him because his personal issues had gotten too hard to handle. He lashed out at you. Even knowing you couldn't help him, even accepting that he didn't want help, you still felt like you abandoned him. I know that, not just because you told me, but because you still talk about it in your sleep. The only thing that calms you is gently stroking your cheek. I never told you that I do that or asked why it works. I think, I may be afraid that you'll say he used to do it when you were low.

[17] My friend said this might be indicative that you were tempted to ask for a threesome. I'd have said no, by the way. Not as a general rule, but because it was your ex. And more importantly, an ex that hurt you. A lot.

[18] It was drugs, Josh. And you were in control. So yes, you ejected him from your life due to a biological incident.

The call screen switched from the usual mix of hold music and relaxing images—in this case a terrible auto-generated version of *Fur Elise* and some stock footage of fish—to the smiling face of a woman.

"Thornton-Hythe legal communications, Ailuros section, Mrs. Banks speaking."

Somehow, the company had found someone that hit every idea of 'generic legal team member' that Sarah had in her head. A projected, expensive looking suit. Neatly tied back blonde ponytail. Librarian glasses. Self-assuredness that bordered dangerously on arrogance and self-appointed supremacy. Her entire demeanour screamed 'welcome to the elite, you can look but you can't touch.'[15]

Sarah cleared her throat. "Hello, Mrs. Banks. This is Miss Walker of Salvagers Guild Three."

"Ah, yes. I understand you've found our abandoned[16] twenty-third unit?"

Sarah nodded. "One of my teams did, yes. Or two of them. Anyway, under UNID conventions, I needed to speak to you all. We're legally allowed to salvage any derelict, but as traceable owners of a commercial property, we need to offer you the opportunity to negotiate a cut of the profits.[17] Or to claim specific items critical to the data safety compliance and general running of your business."

Mrs. Banks smiled. It was a tick-box exercise in sweetness and polite-ness. And entirely fake. "Of course. You'll be happy to know though that we do not intend to claim anything in relation to this unit."

Sarah narrowed her eyes and locked her fingers together, letting them tap the backs of her hands. "Really? If you don't mind me saying, that's not the normal response."

"Are you aware why we lost the unit in the first place?"

Sarah sat back into her chair and crossed her arms, running through what little she knew of the incident in her head. "I remember the news reports. There was some sort of outbreak, and it was ejected as a result, right?"

Mrs. Banks nodded. "To be more precise, there was a biological incident, and the unit commander made the decision to eject the unit.[18] We received no further communication from the unit, and so it was left to float." She shrugged. "Look at this from our standpoint. The only things we'd need to recover would

[19] <The concept of replacing expenditure here may be indicative that the subject feels like they're missing something, and is seeking it elsewhere.>

If that's true here, it means that I either didn't satisfy you, or that there was something he did that I don't. I hate that thought. So fuck you for making me think it.

[20] <Given that the subject is suspected of infidelity, in this case with an ex-lover, this is a possible indicator that he feels as though he never truly came to terms with the reasons for the cessation of the prior relationship.>

You always did flip between blaming him and yourself.

[21] <Under the circumstances, this would appear to be the subject acknowledging that he knew on some level that what he had with his ex was 'dead'. The use of the word 'viral' is also possibly a sign that he knew the relationship was itself unhealthy.>

You're reiterating to yourself that you don't still love him. That's a good sign, really. It means you didn't want to fall into a destructive relationship again. Self-care is important.

be data logs, but they were stored on the central servers, anyway. We've already paid compensation to the families affected, and replaced the unit itself—staff and patrons included—so what else could we possibly want with it?"

"There's the scrap value of the items aboard. That could replace some of your expenditure[19]."

"There's no need. Our insurance is robust."

Sarah sighed. She hated when people viewed other humans as assets. "Well, that makes it easier, I suppose. With regards to the biological incident though, can you tell me anything about it?"

"We know about as much as most, I'm afraid. We never did get a full report[20] on the incident. I can't think of a single currently active viral strain that wouldn't have died out by now though, if that's what you're worried about[21]."

"That was my thinking too. Okay. Thank you for your time, Mrs. Banks."

"Not all. Happy salvaging."

[22] Married. Married a little over a year. I don't know whether to take this as a subconscious attempt at minimizing the relationship. Marriage was a huge thing for me. You kinda just went with it. Maybe you don't differentiate. I suppose we shouldn't really. Relationships have boundaries, and marriage shouldn't alter those. Still. It was a dream for me.

[23] Sadly, yes, it does. We've both had it at work, and that's caused a lot of stress. Mostly due to our differing ways of dealing with it. I know you had to talk to HR about what your line manager said during your end-of-year review. I thought it was a minor argument but maybe it hit you harder than I thought. Or maybe that's just me trying to make excuses for you.

[24] <This is a common piece of imagery. A person having their Skin Suit powered down is a symbol for them being a blank slate in terms of how they're processing the event the Alleviation Sim is dealing with. No masks, no disguises, just preparation for the journey.>

In reality, of course, we make full use of them. All the time. The Skin Suit system is awesome, I think we both agree on that. It makes it easier for us all to slip into those public masks we have at times, and just be ourselves at others. Here, it ties in with the individuation concept mentioned earlier though. I wonder what your 'self' will look like in the end.

SARAH WALKER: You said I could ask questions, didn't you?

MARK TYLER: I did.

SARAH WALKER: In that case, can you tell me what relevance the first recording has to any of this?

MARK TYLER: In cases such as this, we need to establish as clear a picture as possible as it pertains to the people involved. The makeup of the team is particularly important, including their interpersonal relations. Alex and Josh seem close.

SARAH WALKER: They should. They've been dating[22] for a little over a year. Again though, that's irrelevant.

MARK TYLER: Not necessarily. Even now, people can be set off by all sorts of things. Archaic as it may be, bigotry is still a thing, even out here.[23] They call this an enlightened age; I call it same old humans, far bigger reach. Plus, as I'm sure you're aware, we do strange things for love. Tell me, do Josh and Alex cohabit on The Wanderer? I ran a background check but couldn't find a registered planetary address for either of them?

SARAH WALKER: Yes, they live on the ship. And they make sure they follow the guidelines on long-term ship living, too. I monitor that personally as part of their Guild membership.

MARK TYLER: Yes, I see from your reports that they make regular stops to free centrifugal gravity hotspots. Is there a reason that they don't have their Skin Suits powered on full time?[24] I noticed Josh's was off, and the ship scans show that Alex's was the same.

SARAH WALKER: They're careful with money.

MARK TYLER: The constant charge is fairly power efficient. Are they that poor?

SARAH WALKER: No, but they aren't as comfortable as some others either.

[25] I thought about whether we argued that day. We didn't, or not that I can remember, anyway. I suspect it was a trying one for you though. You obviously planned it to some extent, or you wouldn't have sent me to the Comic Con. If you'd checked the site you would have known I wouldn't get in though. Maybe you felt guilty and that's why it was trying. Or maybe you knew I'd come back, and you wanted to get caught, and the potential consequences of that stressed you out. I don't know.

They prefer to play it safe, that's all. A small savings is still
a saving.

MARK TYLER: True enough. Moving on, it sounded like Aaron Colt and
Lucy Foster complain quite often.

SARAH WALKER: What makes you say that?

MARK TYLER: You opened with, "What's the problem now?"

SARAH WALKER: That wasn't for them specifically. They don't complain any
more than most. It was a trying day,[25] that's all. Theirs was
the third escalated issue I'd had to deal with that hour.

MARK TYLER: That sounds tough.

SARAH WALKER: [Shrugs] Part of the job.

MARK TYLER: Can you tell me why you felt the need to warn Aaron and
Lucy not to start any trouble?

SARAH WALKER: Because Alex and Josh are not their favourite people.
Lucy Foster knows the rules well enough to know just
how far she can push it without getting herself in trouble.
She is not, however, above pushing people's buttons. My
worry was that she was angry enough to try pushing one or
both of them into getting themselves suspended.

MARK TYLER: Is that something she does often? Not just with Alex and
Josh, in general I mean.

SARAH WALKER: Allegedly. I've never found any usable evidence to confirm it.

MARK TYLER: And without evidence, you can't act.

SARAH WALKER: Other than to investigate complaints, no.

MARK TYLER: I personally find that those wishing to cause the most
trouble are the ones that are the most careful.

SARAH WALKER: [Nods]

MARK TYLER: In terms of the communication with Thornton-Hythe, you
acknowledged that it was unusual for a company not to

[26] <Given the circumstances, this is likely all sexual. Active viral strains dying out relates to old relationships. Minor doubt about which was involved is potentially more to do with emotions and how the subject felt about his ex. Residual infection is a reigniting of old feelings, and the risks involved with recovery is what would happen if he acted on those feelings.>

[27] <Working to the same concept, the mechanisms are to avoid the relevant negative behaviours.>

Does that mean your eyes stray a lot, I wonder? I would hope that the 'mechanism' is love. Ugh. I'm romanticizing this. It'll be guilt, or morals. Whatever. Sometimes, mechanisms break. I don't mind you thinking people are hot. It's acting on it that causes problems.

[28] <Assuming the event being dealt with here is the infidelity, this is a strong indicator that the subject has either cheated or been tempted to before. If the Ailuros unit relates purely to this instance, then this means that at least one instance of prior cheating (or temptation to) relates to his current partner.>

That hurt. The thing is, interpretation applies here to an extent. But let me make this very clear. Whether you physically cheated, or whether this was temptation, I know what I saw. I'm clinging to the hope that you didn't go much further than what I witnessed, but the fact is, you were all over him for that moment. To me, that's cheating.

[29] <An in built sense of self-preservation. The subject would not directly give away things that have happened before, partially because they aren't entirely relevant, but also because they may have already dealt with it internally.>

[30] You thought that I cheated on you, shortly after the wedding. I still remember the nights with us both in tears. I accused you of projecting your own guilt on me. I truly am sorry for that. I was angry. If that's what pushed you into this, I am every bit as terrible a person as you said I am.

want a cut of the salvage. Why did you not push this point further?

SARAH WALKER: Because it's unusual, but not unheard of. I thought that her wording was fairly smart too. 'I can't think of a single currently active viral strain that wouldn't have died out by now,' indicated to me that there was some minor doubt about what virus was involved. I figured that she wanted to cover the Ailuros project's back with regards to any residual infection that we may contract by salvaging. And avoid risking their staff by recovering the items.[26]

MARK TYLER: Did that not worry you?

SARAH WALKER: To a point. But we're salvagers. The fact is, we rarely know the full story going into a job. We risk things like that every time we enter a derelict. To that end, we have mechanisms to avoid infection.[27]

MARK TYLER: [Nods] Would it surprise you to hear that you may not have been the first to find the unit?[28]

SARAH WALKER: [Tensing] Excuse me?

MARK TYLER: I can't divulge any information, of course, data security being what it is.[29] However, there is some evidence that an independent salvager may have previously entered the unit. We are investigating this and the possibility that information was intentionally withheld when you contacted Mrs. Banks.

SARAH WALKER: When you say 'we,' do you mean you?

MARK TYLER: No. I am involved, but not in an investigatory manner, largely due to the case being linked with another that I am legally barred from investigating.

SARAH WALKER: Barred. Why?

MARK TYLER: Because the independent salvager is…*was*…my husband.[30]

SARAH WALKER: [Nods and starts to speak but stops herself.] How does that affect the investigation into our Guild?

MARK TYLER: In terms of the core elements of the investigation, it doesn't. There was no way you could have known what

 I think I was right. You're acknowledging that it's not the only reason here, but our issues did play into it. I suppose that should have been obvious. Healthy relationships don't involve things like drugging your partner and psychoanalyzing their Waking Dreams, do they? What happened to us, Josh? Were we always like this?

would happen, even if information was not withheld. Of course, the cases will be linked up in the end, but their interactions at this point is minimal.[31]

SARAH WALKER: Then why bring it up at all?

MARK TYLER: Technically, telling you this contravenes at least one rule, but you seemed guarded. That's understandable. I just thought you would find some solace in knowing that we're looking into all potential wrongdoing. And that you aren't the only one suffering due to this incident. The main point, Sarah, is that this isn't aimed squarely at yourselves. Any way, let's move on to what happened after Josh and Alex arrived.

[32] We're kinda opposites in reality, I think. You moved from instability to stability. I moved from stable relationships to what we have. The use of the word 'simulated' matters most here, I think. You used to tell me that you were worried that we were combustible, but pretending that things were fine. I always replied that you were being silly, and that it was all an overreaction based on how things used to be for you. Looking at it now, I was being unfair. I guess that certainty that I hung onto was as real as the false gravity of a spinning space station.

[33] <This is part of the 'bringing things together' process. The different facts of the subject are forced into a 'uniform' to make them easier to recognize.>

[34] I smiled when I read that. My gender identity is important to me. I know that not everyone gets it. A lot of people don't think 'genderfluid' is a real thing. They say it's attention seeking. At my age too, it's worse, because people think I'm, at best, just trying to play along with the teenagers and, at worst, trying to find a way to sneak into women's bathrooms. Laws and general acceptance help, but like you said, bigotry still exists. That you placed some importance on my identity in this is wonderful. It's all subconscious too, which means you accept it fully. So, thank you for that.

Alex stretched their arms. Stepping from the microgravity environment they had become used to living in into the simulated gravity of Salvagers Guild Three's rotating HQ always made their stomach flip a little.[32]

Both their and Josh's Skin Suits automatically synched up with the HQ wireless charge and data stream, overriding their settings for the duration of their visit. That meant that they switched instantly from their regular 'off' setting to projecting the guild uniform[33] the moment they stepped on board.

Alex didn't mind that though. The uniform was simple enough: a form-fitting one-piece that offered only slight variances in colour, and some light-up sections should it be needed on a salvage. It was basically a homage to pre-space colony sci-fi television.

It was unisex though, which meant that Alex could feel comfortable no matter how they felt that day without needed to make tiresome projection switches. That was important.[34] The one exception to the auto-synch was hair. In that regard, Alex got to keep their neatly shaven, dark sides and short, choppy, rainbow-tipped spikes.

Alex walked just a little ahead of Josh as they entered the bar. The chatter remained constant, as it always did, but the glances that people gave them were noticeable. Alex knew that Josh saw them too, that's why they started taking the lead during visits; seeing their Puss-Puss getting visibly agitated by it all was stressful. For both of them.

As they neared the back of the room, a large shape stepped out in front of them, blocking their path. Alex looked up, unsurprised to see Aaron Colt staring down at them, his chest puffed out, and untoned, but imposingly large, arms swaying as though unsure where to swing at first. With his shortly shaven hair projection, he looked every bit the thug that he was.

"I hear you stole our score," he said, his lips pulling back in disgust.

Alex glanced over at Lucy Foster, who had positioned herself behind Aaron, with an unsettling smirk on her face. They looked back to Aaron and involuntarily tensed up. "I don't know what you're talking about."

"Oh, I think you do, shithead," Aaron replied, leaning forward to loom over Alex. "Ailuros."

Alex felt a hand on their shoulder, and Josh pulled them back, stepping

[35] <We're going to get a little Freudian here, but Aaron is likely representative of the subject's Id. He is pure aggression and impulse. While the subject's dream self responds in a protective way, they are still also acting aggressively. It could be that they feel controlled by their basic urges, or it could be that they feel like they are constantly fighting them. The Id is usually controlled by the Ego. Lucy appears to be framed as setting Aaron on this path, which would place her in that role. The Ego is directly influenced by the real world and forces the Id to step in line, but with the overall goal of getting what it wants without negative consequences, so that fits. That she acts so manipulatively is a worry though. Healthy minds are often led by the Ego, but she seems to be a potentially more destructive force than she should be.>

'Take what you want, when you want it.' That was the life he offered you. And you tried to embrace it a little. Not entirely, but enough to see that it had positives. We talked about that. You knew that living so selfishly was wrong, but there was an allure to it. Maybe that's what this is; there's a lot of aggression on display, so your Ego is acting out to force things in line while still embracing that little piece of selfishness. I don't know. I don't really understand all of this, hence getting my friend involved. All I can really do is relate things to the real world. That's apparently important though. Even with a rigid framework for analysis, personal traits should be applied to get a clear picture.

[36] It's like you don't truly understand what happened. Even if it's a repeated offense, the way the Neg-Vacs work mean that none of us have to deal with certain impulses openly anymore. But you don't get them, so you're kinda stuck in this cycle of staring them in the face with nobody around you to relate to in terms of how you feel about them. Neg-Vacs. Maybe they're not as good a thing as we're sometimes told. Do Alleviation Sims really allow us to deal with stuff like this? Do we have a duty to other people to not use them so that those who don't have access to this 'miracle tool' still have a means to communicate what they're feeling? The way I brushed off your concerns as silly is partly to blame, isn't it? Or am I just projecting it on myself because I don't want to accept the idea that you're a bad person?

protectively between the two of them. He was in visibly better shape than Aaron, but still slightly shorter, meaning he needed to look up as he asked, "Do you really want to do this here?"

Colt snapped his hand out and grabbed Josh's shirt, pulling him in close and forcing him up on the balls of his feet.[35] The room fell silent bar the music playing over the speakers, and Aaron smiled, spit dripping from his teeth as he growled, "Ya know what? I think I do."

Alex held their breath, noticing Josh ball his hand into a fist. They didn't exhale until the sound of Sarah Walker's voice cut through the conflict. "Aaron, that's enough! Alex! Josh! In here, now!"

Sarah let her door slide shut without waiting to see what would happen. Her confidence in that being the end of it was clear. She was well-respected enough, even among the more combustible members of the Guild, that everyone tended to just follow what she said.

Colt dropped Josh and grumbled quietly, "Ya got lucky."

Not content with that as a parting shot, he took the time to shove Josh as he passed. Alex was glad to see that Josh's only response was a glare and a stern point of his finger.

Once inside Sarah's office, Alex took up position in one of the two chairs that Sarah pointed too. Josh sat beside them, still visibly angry, and said, "That was not our fault."

Sarah waved the comment away and got straight to the point. "You two have got quite the find here, haven't you? What do you know about the unit?"

"Only that it was ejected from the main station," Alex replied. "The press didn't really say much else at the time other than that it was due to some sort of outbreak."

"Well, I did a little digging while you were en route. Ailuros told me it was a biological incident but didn't clarify what exactly. They did say that it should be fine to salvage now though."[36]

Alex nodded. "And how much of a cut do they want?"

"None. The data logs were stored centrally, and they've already replaced the physical unit and paid reparations to the families of those still on board during ejection. As far as they're concerned, they've washed their hands of it."

Alex shared a glance with Josh.

Josh crossed his arms and frowned. "That doesn't sound right."

"No, it does not," Sarah agreed. "Normally, a traceable owner would want to recover whatever the UN Abandonment Laws would allow. Given the nature of the ejection though, there are potential risks involved. They never did find

[37] Abandonment, risks, never finding out what happened. You fear that I'll leave you. And no, it doesn't sound right. None of this, neither your actions or mine, are 'right.'

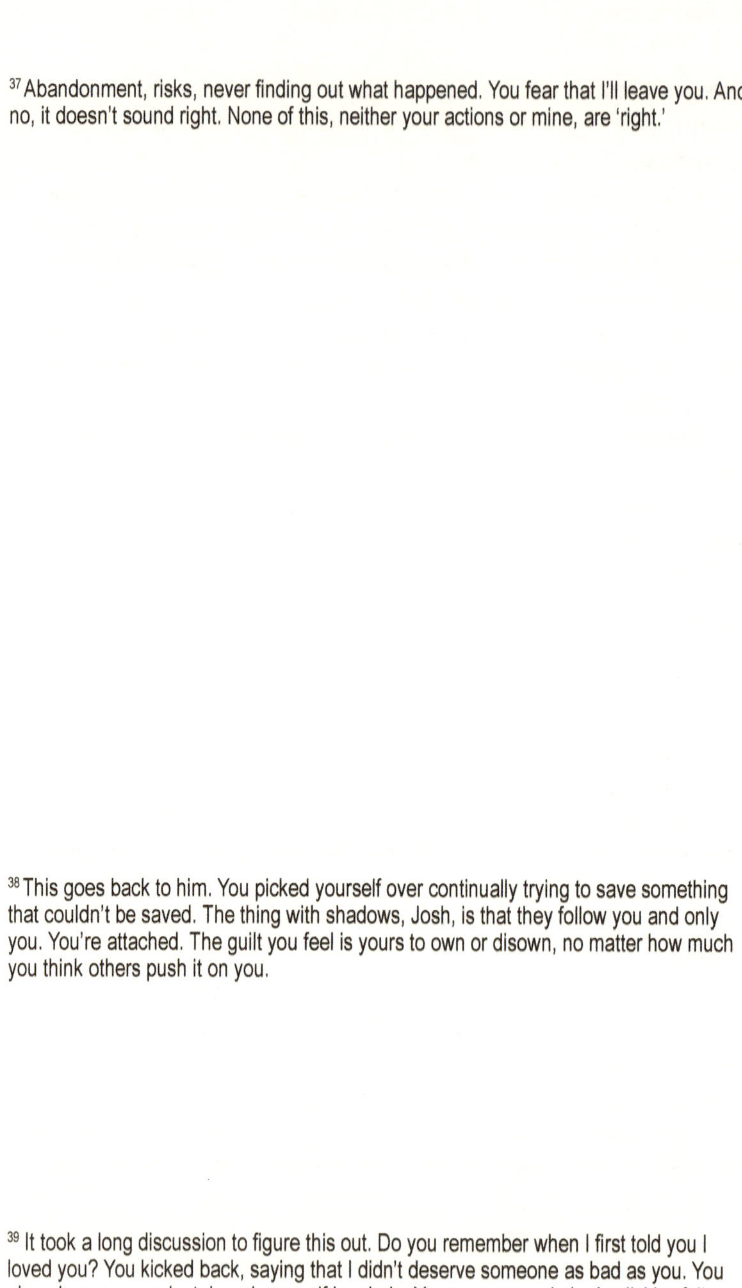

[38] This goes back to him. You picked yourself over continually trying to save something that couldn't be saved. The thing with shadows, Josh, is that they follow you and only you. You're attached. The guilt you feel is yours to own or disown, no matter how much you think others push it on you.

[39] It took a long discussion to figure this out. Do you remember when I first told you I loved you? You kicked back, saying that I didn't deserve someone as bad as you. You placed me on a pedestal, and yourself in a hole. You were scared, that's all. You fell hard and didn't think you were good enough. That wasn't helped by others pointing out your reputation to me. In front of you. It took a while for you to realize that feelings of inadequacy is something we all feel sometimes. None of us are perfect, and nobody sees it more clearly than ourselves.

out what exactly happened there after all."[37]

Sarah sighed and added, "It does happen sometimes though. And I can't justify letting something this big go, so you've got your approval. Providing you agree to working with a couple of other teams."

letting something this big go, so you've got your approval. Providing you agree to working with a couple of other teams."

Josh felt the anger rise into his face in a flash of red. He rose to his feet and snapped, "Oh, come on! You saw—"

"Sit down, Josh," Sarah said. It was stern, but not nearly as aggressive as she had been when breaking up the potential fight. Josh needed to be ordered to do things sometimes, but he was nowhere near the trouble that some could be.

When Josh finally sat down, ceding the battle of wills, Sarah continued, "You do realize how big that thing is, right? There's no way you can do a thorough job on your own. Besides, this might help mend some bridges. The last thing you want is to foster more bad blood out there."

"Bad blood," Josh grunted. "Fuck them."

"Really? Because to a lot of them, you're still just the greedy bastard that picked the score over his partner."

Josh recoiled. "That's not fair."

"Do you think I don't know that?" Sarah groaned. "I went over those logs five times. And I made damn sure that the rest of the Guild knew what the official ruling was. That doesn't stop them thinking it though. We're all followed by our shadows Josh, even out here."[38]

Alex placed their hand on Josh's shoulder, giving it a reassuring squeeze.

"And you're not excluded from this either," Sarah added, responding to the action. "Even if you weren't working with Josh here, you're openly listed as staff for two large Earth-hosted companies. All the time that's the case, you're going to be seen as the rich kid playing salvager."

Alex sighed and rubbed their eyes. "My father's companies have been hemorrhaging money for years. I may be listed as director for two of them, but that's in name only, and only so he can comply with regulations. Plus, I'm non-remunerative. He can't afford to pay me."

"I'm aware of that, Alex. The fact is, most of them out there don't care. You have to understand; most salvagers have had to drag themselves up and take every little win they can get. They look at you, and they don't see that your family did the same. They just see your father's previous success.[39] It's that simple. And neither of you have dealt with the conflicts particularly well. My

[40] You clearly view Sarah as the ideal. She's balanced in what she does and says, and you're describing her as being very strong in different ways. You also view her as what you think I want. I'm assuming she represents what you want to give me. The thing is, you're not entirely right. How capable she is would be nice, but only because I want to see you being able to cope, not because I don't think you're enough. Like I said, we're all imperfect. I like imperfections.

hope is that if you—both of you—work with a few of them, they'll all see that you're worth more than their complaining."

Josh crossed his arms, his defiance showing through. "We called this in. It should be our job."

"It will be. You'll be the leads. The others will be there to help, not take over. Eighty percent of the profit gets split evenly between all of you, and the other twenty goes six percent to you and fourteen to the Guild. Same as any joint operation with set command percent to you and fourteen to the Guild. Same as any joint operation with set command structure."

"Fine," Josh replied. "Who are you sticking us with?"

"Rob and Alice Kemble will be your seconds. I also want you to take Aaron Colt and Lucy Foster with you."

Josh laughed, and Alex tensed at the sound. It wasn't a good laugh. It also meant that they needed to speak first before Josh said something he'd regret. "I don't think I've ever spoken to the Kembles, but Colt and Foster? They accused us of stealing this job. I know you heard that."

"That's why I'm sending them with you," Sarah replied. She tapped her desk display and called up a side-by-side comparison of the derelict scan logs from both The Wanderer and Foster's Hope. "Their logs show that they technically did find the Ailuros unit first, they just got lazy with the paperwork. Think of it as building good will."

Alex nodded. "The Kembles, Colt, and Foster. Okay. Anybody else?"

"Yeah, I'll be sending some rookies along with you too. Stuart Grant and Kevin Stockley. Stuart should be pretty useful; he used to work on Ailuros. And while I wouldn't make him your first choice, Kevin is technically a registered pilot, so he should be a good back-up. He's only ever flown small haul ships before though, so maybe give him a crash course in the finer points of piloting if you get the chance?"

"I assume we're taking one of the bigger ships then?" Josh asked, raising a curious eyebrow.

"I'm giving you The Orca for this one. It's not the newest ship we have on hand, but it's the most useful for what you're going to need to do. Now. Let's go gather your team and get this started."

Sarah rose to her feet, and Alex watched her military-style jacket flutter as she stretched. It was a majestic animation routine. Subtle, but majestic. She clearly understood the point of aesthetics and how it played a part in the feel she gave off. That was important.[40]

[41] It's taken me until to now to fully register the concept of hair projections. We only have clothing projections in reality. It makes sense though. In microgravity, hair would go all over the place. Keeping it shaven with a projection to provide individuality seems like a good compromise. I don't think it means anything here other than that your brain is creative.

<This is a fair comment. Sometimes, an image or idea is just that, with no hidden meaning or agenda. The human brain is built to create. Though, in this instance, the comment is wrong. Though rarely remembered, Hair Projections are programmed into the Alleviation Sims.>

Alice Kemble leant back against the door to The Orca and crossed her arms. She shook her head to the side, forcing the projection of her mousey bangs to react and flip back over her ears. Realism in the projections was a good thing, but she often wondered why they kept the more bothersome side of reality ingrained in the programming.[41]

She was watching Sarah as she observed the room, catching the odd glance here and there. Alice smiled and tapped her arm, making sure Sarah knew that she knew what she was looking at: she had opted for the short sleeve version of the uniform, entirely to show off her latest homebrew experiment.

The tribal snake tattoo on Alice's arm glowed and writhed around. It was following a set path along her arm, essentially moving on rails. Untampered tattoo projections were designed to mimic the real thing. That meant static designs. This was a lot more fun. After all, if you were gonna wear tech-clothes, why wouldn't you experiment.

"Next stop, free roaming designs," she mumbled.

Next to Alice, her brother, Rob, let out a quiet laugh. "You winding Sarah up again?"

"Distracting her," I think.

"It's a good thing Ronnie doesn't mind you messing with her sister. She would totally wreck you if you pissed her off."

Alice shrugged. "I only get away with it because I don't take it as far as you do."

Rob smiled. "Humour. It's too bloody subjective."

"Okay people, this is a big one," Sarah said, drawing the attention of the room. "Ailuros Unit Twenty-Three is an abandoned leisure destination. It contains living quarters, the usual maintenance and managerial sections, and a whole selection of holiday activities. Given the size of the target, I'm implementing a command structure for the salvage. Leading the mission are Alex Holden and Josh Byrne. Seconds are Rob and Alice Kemble. Next, Aaron Colt and Lucy Foster. If all else fails, Kevin Stockely and Stuart Grant."

Aaron crossed his arms and grinned, obviously very pleased about what he planned to say. "Any reason we ain't in charge, given we found the thing

[42] <Alice trying to assert control over Aaron—the Id—and get his aggression under control may mark her as the Superego. She even brought it back around to sex, which is a fundamental part of the Id.>

[43] I wish the Skin Suits could really do that. It would be so much easier than using breast forms. You're right though. I may have been born male, but I feel more confident when I'm feeling female. You never asked, but believe it or not, I did consider GRS for a while. With the way my self-identity changes though, I decided against it. I don't feel fully one gender, not permanently. I choose to embrace that and let myself slide along the scale whenever I need to without trying to force myself into one box or another. So, there's some honesty for you, and something you didn't know about me. It would feel unfair if I was the only one learning.

and all? Oh, wait, let me guess. We're piggy-backing the rich kid's insurance, right?"

"There are plenty of reasons, Colt," Sarah replied, keeping her eyes forward rather than dignifying the comment with a physical acknowledgement. "For one, nobody else here tried to start a fight in the bar tonight. Not to mention that you didn't get the official claim because you couldn't be bothered to report in when you found the thing. Laziness is not a good quality in a leader."here tried to start a fight in the bar tonight. Not to mention that you didn't get the official claim because you couldn't be bothered to report in when you found the thing. Laziness is not a good quality in a leader."

"Yeah?" Aaron shrugged and turned toward Josh Byrne, who was standing to the side of Sarah with his partner. "Last I checked, nor is causing the death of a salvage partner."

Alice noticed Josh bristle at the comment and made a conscious decision to not let Aaron Colt push this the wrong way. "Jesus Christ, Colt," she cut in. "You really don't know when to shut up, do you?"

"What's that supposed to mean?" he replied, unable to keep the surprise at someone speaking up out of his voice.

"It means, the longer you spend trying to start a fight, the longer this takes," Rob said, joining the fun.

Alice nodded. "Exactly. I have a wife to get back to."

Aaron turned to face the Kembles, fist clenched and face reddening. "Yeah? And the only reason you have a wife is that she ain't met me yet."

Alice rolled her eyes. "Uh-huh. I know you have a face built for Incel Dating Apps, but have you ever considered that maybe, if you stopped acting like a dick, someone might pay attention to yours?"[42]

Clang!

The whole room turned to face Sarah who, apparently sick of the brewing conflict, had slammed her fist against a nearby crate. "Enough! Alex, will you please run through what they need to know?"

Alex stepped forward and, under the light, Alice noticed that something had changed about the salvager. When they walked through the bar, they looked masculine. A touch androgynous maybe, but definitely male. Now, their Skin Suit had adapted and crated the illusion of a clearly female chest. Their walk had changed too, and their posture. They seemed more self-assured.[43]

"Ailuros Unit Twenty-Three was ejected from the main body two and a half years ago," Alex began. "Though the news sites declared it a non-defined outbreak, the official reason is listed more specifically as a biological incident.

We don't have any other details with regards to that, so we need to play things safe. Sarah has allocated us The Orca for the salvage and signed off on enough oxygen for us all to suit up for a full day and a half, provided we run shifts."

"What sort of salvage are we expecting?" Alice asked.

"We aren't sure. According to the inventory supplied by the owning body, we should be able to find plenty of high-grade—albeit outdated—electronic parts. Given the nature of the place, I'm expecting plenty of smaller items in the living quarters. The main thing is, nobody involved with Ailuros wants a cut, so we're getting a solid twenty percent per team."

Rob relaxed at the confirmation of pay and commented, "Sounds normal for a commercial derelict. Anything else we need to know?"

"The unit was fully manned when it was ejected," Josh confirmed. "Staff and guests. Expect bodies."

"Anybody important enough for us to empty the freezer?"

It would be hard not to pick up on the cold detachment in Lucy's voice when she asked the question. It was a fair one though. The rookies clearly weren't expecting it, but they would grow to, over time.

Alex cleared their throat, breaking the silence. "No. Nobody aboard was an anybody. They were all just everyday people. As far as we know."

"Standard rules apply," Sarah clarified. "If you find someone unexpected, call it in, and I'll seek guidance from the relevant legal bodies. Otherwise, focus on the normal salvage."

Alex took a deep breath and exhaled. "The pre-launch checks have already been run, so I suggest we get on board and head out."

Alice swung one arm over her shoulder, hitting the door release button without looking. The doors to The Orca slid open, and she smiled. "Sounds good to me."

MARK TYLER: So, what did you think of all of that?

SARAH WALKER: [Shrugs] I think you probably have some questions.

MARK TYLER: [Nods] I do, yes. With regards to Aaron Colt, is his aggression here normal?

SARAH WALKER: He likes to push buttons, yes. While he was a little more overt with it than normal, he was angry about losing the brunt of the salvage. That's understandable.

MARK TYLER: Is that why you didn't pull him up on it?

SARAH WALKER: To a point. When under my direct control, I give my staff a single warning out of courtesy. If they cut back on what they're doing—as Aaron Colt did here—then I let it slide. Frankly though, I'm not a babysitter. While this was supposed to help Alex and Josh mend bridges, all Guild members need to learn to get along.

MARK TYLER: Makes sense. Still, it was sneaky of Lucy Foster, don't you think?

SARAH WALKER: Giving her word not to start trouble herself, but not mentioning Colt, you mean? Yes, it was. It's frustrating that I didn't notice that when she made the promise.

MARK TYLER: You could argue that sneaky is an apt term for her though, couldn't you? And not just with the promise here, or the rumours of misconduct. Were you aware that she has a son?

SARAH WALKER: Steven, yes. And yes, I know where he is.

MARK TYLER: Staying at Her Majesty's pleasure. The charges were arson and manslaughter, having intentionally started a fire at their home that inadvertently killed his father, Daniel Crowe. He claimed to have started the blaze after an argument with Daniel regarding a drinking issue.

SARAH WALKER: And?

[44] Reading this, I'm more certain of Sarah being what you view as the ideal. She is fair in how she deals with things, but is naturally trying to rationalize things in order to give leeway. At the same time, Mark too is an ideal of sorts. More cold than Sarah in some ways, but also more fragile in others. Perhaps it's a balance you want to achieve?

<Were I approaching this using Carl Jung as a basis, I would place them as the subject's Anima and Animus, seeking to come together to form the Syzygy, or divine couple. That does tie in with the subject using them as proxies to work through issues too. I will mostly stick with Freud for core elements here, but I won't discount others' studies either. The human mind is far too complex for a blanket approach to work in all cases.>

MARK TYLER: Well, there are rumours that Lucy and her son conspired to murder, aren't there?

SARAH WALKER: Yes, there are. Based around the idea that Lucy was an abusive partner and, after getting him to change his will, acted to make gains from it. There are also rumours that Daniel was an abusive partner and, after seeing him hit his mother, Steven took matters into his own hands, setting the fire afterward to gain a reduced sentence. Rumours exist. Would you like to know some facts?

MARK TYLER: Sure.

SARAH WALKER: One, the matter was dealt with by the law, and so, even if I believed the rumours that she killed Daniel, I would be unable to act on them. So, don't you dare try pushing that angle. Two, Lucy had it tough growing up. She has had to lash out from an early age because it was the only way to survive. Her ship, Foster's Hope, was named because she viewed it as a way to create a better life for herself and her child.

MARK TYLER: Could you not also say that it is a fact that Daniel Crowe began the process of pressing charges against Lucy multiple times, each file accompanied by photographs of his injuries though? I noted that there were no instances of Lucy filing charges.

SARAH WALKER: Yes, you could. You could also say that it is a fact that many people, men and women, don't feel able to report instances of domestic abuse for a whole number of reasons ranging from outright manipulation to a history—whether personal or local—of such claims not being believed. Whatever logic you want to apply to the situation though, at this point it would simply be guesswork. When it comes to that case though, do you know what the most important fact is?

MARK TYLER: No.

SARAH WALKER: It's this. I know Lucy Foster. She is a lot of things, some of them very unpleasant, but she is not capable of murder.[44]

MARK TYLER: I see. Well, I apologize for the upset. Please try to under stand though that I need to look at things from all angles

[45] The peer review group represents my friends, doesn't it? Did you really feel that way about the way my friends interfered with us at the start? I suppose you would. The trouble was, when you dated him, a lot of your clashes were in public, and even with him clearly being in the wrong a lot of the time, you weren't a saint in the whole mess either. Not to mention your actions with partners afterwards. Is it cruel to bring it all up now?

[46] Macey represents your ex, I suppose he was popular. From what you told me, when he had good days, he was the life of the party. And when he had bad days, people felt bad for him. Even more so when you started lashing out. I don't blame you about that, by the way. I never did. I understand how complicated it was.

[47] My choice to date you was unpopular, *I* wasn't. But the pushback did make me more determined to make it work. I don't want to view that as an error, even if I stuck with you partly due to stubbornness. Honestly, I thought we were working. We had to work at working sometimes, but that happens, right?

to ascertain what exactly happened here. That does mean touching on some unfortunate points.

SARAH WALKER: [Takes a deep breath and exhales] I know. I know that. Just...let's get on with it.

MARK TYLER: Okay. I won't ask for the full details, we still have the report on hand from when it happened. As it was mentioned multiple times though, can you briefly summarize why some members of the Guild have a low opinion of Josh Byrne?

SARAH WALKER: [Groans] About a year and a half ago, he and his previous salvage partner, Macey, were sent to look at an old war ship on a planetary body. It seemed safe enough to work with, but worsening conditions on the surface meant they encountered some unexpected issues. Macey died, Josh survived. Like I said on the video, I played back the logs multiple times and had a full peer review group study them too. Josh was not at fault. If he hadn't taken any of the salvage, he probably wouldn't be viewed the way he is though.[45]

MARK TYLER: Okay. And Alex...no, actually, let's move on a little. You mentioned bad blood and mending bridges. Have Alex and Josh not tried to do so before?

SARAH WALKER: Josh was hurt by what happened and wasn't without guilt. Macey was popular, too.[46] When people lashed out, he took it for a while, then started returning it in kind. You saw how he responded to Colt. When he, or someone he cares about is threatened, he tends to act aggressively. Alex was unpopular from the start, that's probably why the two of them initially gravitated toward each other.[47] Alex is far quieter than Josh though, and more prone to just shutting things out.

MARK TYLER: Ah, so they ended up distancing themselves in multiple ways.

SARAH WALKER: Yes.

MARK TYLER: In the hangar, it wasn't just Josh and Alex who had issues with Colt, though. Alice seemed very unhappy with his conduct. What interested me was that she mentioned she has a wife, Ronnie. It took a little while to figure out, as

[48] We certainly didn't, did we?

[49] And not entirely different to how we met, is it? I was meeting up with my brother after a particularly shitty day at work and he was running late. I saw you there at the bar, and you looked, I don't know. Mysterious, I suppose? You were smiling, but it was fragile. But still a beautiful smile. I wanted to make your smile strong. Was I trying to save you before knowing what you were running from? Maybe. Anyway, my brother turned up later, saw us together, and left me to it. He was actually our strongest supporter from the get-go.

neither of them took the other's surname, but she's married to your sister, isn't she?

SARAH WALKER: Not every couple has to pick and choose, or even double barrel a surname, you know.[48] Yes, though, she and Ronnie have been together for a long time now.

MARK TYLER: Did they meet through you?

SARAH WALKER: [Smiles] Yeah, sort of. Ronnie was meeting me after work for a catch up and got talking to Alice while she was waiting for me to finish up some paperwork. When I saw how well they were getting on, I left them to it.

MARK TYLER: That's sweet.[49] And I'm sorry, but I have to ask. Did your familial connection to Alice influence your decision to place her on this salvage?

SARAH WALKER: No, it did not.

MARK TYLER: [Checks readings] The scanners say otherwise.

SARAH WALKER: [Pauses] I suppose, to a degree, her relationship with my sister did affect my decision, but not in the way you might be thinking. Before I say anything else, can I clarify something?

MARK TYLER: Sure.

SARAH WALKER: Are you insinuating that there was an intentional move on my part to benefit my family members?

MARK TYLER: Not at all. I simply want to understand your thinking when it comes to your choices of crew members here.

SARAH WALKER: [Nods] Okay. It affected my decision insofar as her relationship with my sister meant that I got to know both Alice and Rob better than I otherwise would have.

[Smiles] They even set me and Rob up on a date once, not that anything came from it. Anyway, I knew that there was a possibility of conflict between Alex and Josh, and Aaron and Lucy. I know Alice and Rob well enough to trust that they'd behave in a reasonable manner. My thinking

[50] <The Superego technically has two parts: The conscience, which punishes the Ego if it gives in to the Id's demands, and the Ideal-Self, which represents how to behave as a member of society. Both are important, like a Yin and Yang of sorts. It may be that the subject has literally split them here. Which is which will likely become clear as we progress.>

was that they'd actually listen to the team leads, which would in turn potentially help diffuse conflict and set a good example for the rookies.[50]

MARK TYLER: Did you regret that decision after the back and forth in the hangar?

SARAH WALKER: Of course not. Aaron deserved the backlash. I only stepped in because I didn't want it to go on too long.

MARK TYLER: With regards to the rookies, they actually bring the total number of salvagers above the recommended number in this instance, don't they?

SARAH WALKER: Recommended, not mandated. I like to give rookies a chance to learn from their more experienced colleagues. Here, they'd get that, along with a potentially nice pay out afterward. Plus, the unit is large enough that two extra pairs of hands wouldn't hurt.

MARK TYLER: And the potential conflict with Alex, Josh, Aaron, and Lucy? Was it wise to put them in the middle of that?

SARAH WALKER: It helps it, in a way. Like I said, Lucy knows the rules. Any issues during a salvage would be fully investigated, and having more potential witnesses there would, in theory, help keep her in check. Especially when it's a pair of salvagers that she's not already friendly with.

MARK TYLER: Fair enough. Before we move on, I need to ask you to confirm a few things for me. Is that alright?

SARAH WALKER: [Nods] Go ahead.

MARK TYLER: First, this was the last contact you had with the crew, is that correct?

SARAH WALKER: Yes. Until you brought the emergency signal to me, I didn't hear anything else.

MARK TYLER: That means that the footage we will be reviewing next is unknown to you. By that I mean that you have not seen any of it before now. Is that correct?

SARAH WALKER: That's right.

MARK TYLER: And can you confirm that you have not had any contact
with the crew of The Orca since the incident?

SARAH WALKER: No, I haven't spoken to them. You've all done a wonderful
job of keeping me in the dark.

MARK TYLER: Okay, good. In that case, let's continue.

Alex led the pilots to the bridge and, once inside, asked, "So, who wants to do the honours? Anyone flown The Orca before?"

"I have," Rob replied. "She's no different to most this size, but I'd be happy to set her off."

Alex nodded and Rob moved to the pilot's seat. He started working through screens, coming finally to the launch controls. Moments later, the ship had disengaged from the HQ and was righting itself.

Rob called up the controls and hit the Scent Marker launch button, causing the front of the ship to launch a pyramid ahead of it. Once at a far enough distance, the pyramid split, sending a further part ahead and then, further ahead still, the pyramid split again.

Rob watched the screen, waiting for it all to synch up. Once the screen confirmed communication with the mobile navigation system, he said, "Scent markers deployed and transmitting with a nought point three second delay. Early signs show one incoming body."

Alex floated over and checked the readout. "You may as well let the ship adjust course as it goes. It looks pretty small anyway, and this thing's built to last."

Aaron snorted and tugged at some low hanging cables. "Built to last. You sure about that? Look at this crap. Walker could have at least given us one of the newer ships."

Rob turned his chair, the belt keeping him in place despite the shift to microgravity. "The Ailuros unit's in free roll. The first thing we're going to have to do when we get there is get it back under control. The Orca's the only ship in the Guild with enough raw power to do that quickly."

Aaron smiled and floated over to hover behind Alex. He placed a hand on their shoulder and leaned in close to speak directly in their ear. "Sucks that we can't all just upgrade whenever we want, don't it?"[51]

Rob sighed. "Hey, Colt. Do me a favour."

"Sure."

"Fuck off and find something useful to do."

Aaron chuckled and gave Rob the middle finger. He pushed off Alex's back and left as instructed but made sure to pull random items away from their magnetized holdings on his way, leaving them floating chaotically in the doorway.

[52] I actually figured this one out myself. The most common reason we argued, at least when it was my fault, was that I wouldn't just come out and say what was bothering me. This is you telling me to just come out with it. You're saying that that would help counter the Id-driven side of you. Yet here I am, having drugged you, stolen your report, and shared it with a third party. And why? Because I couldn't just say, "I saw you." The coward in me wants to blame the Neg-Vacs for that. Scream that I couldn't deal with the issues because they suppressed the emotions I needed to embrace to work through it all in the past. I could say that everything that happened here is because the injections caused a build-up that just got too big to contain. But that would be a lie, wouldn't it? If nothing else, this whole experience is really hammering home how much we both need to work at things. See, Josh? I'm not perfect. Not by any stretch of the imagination.

"Thanks," Alex said.

Rob nodded. "Aaron Colt likes to talk. Trust me, all you have to do is tell him what you think without rising to his bait and he'll back off. Let him know you're not interested in fighting, and he's a pushover.[52] His partner, Lucy? Not so much. She's the one you need to watch."

"Really? She always seems…I don't know, quiet?"

"That's the problem. With Aaron, you know what stupid shit he's thinking when he's thinking it because he can't help but blurt it out. Lucy won't make it clear until it's too late. Those two have driven far too many people out of the Guild before now. Try not to let you and Josh be next."

"I was under the impression that there were plenty in the Guild who wouldn't mind if we did get chased out."

"Maybe. I've got no problem with you myself." Rob turned to face Kevin, who had been fidgeting in the corner throughout the confrontation. "Stockley, right?"

"Yeah," he replied. "Kevin. Kevin Stockley."

"Well, Kevin Stockley, do you have any problem with Alex here? Or Josh Byrne?"

Kevin shook his head. "No. I mean, I heard things, but…I don't want to judge anyone without knowing them, you know?"

"Good. Is this your first joint salvage?"

"Second. The last one was only one other team though. It was a much smaller ship, too."

Alex smiled, remembering Sarah's request during their meeting. "Would you like a crash course in how a ship this size works?"

"That would be great!" he yelped, his uneasiness melting away instantly.

⁵³ <Working on the idea that the Ailuros unit is a representation of the subject's sins, this would be a reference to lingering feelings for the person they are suspected of cheating with.>

The more I think about it, the more I'm coming to realize something. I should have told you that it was fine. He had an impact on your life and, even if it ended badly, to still feel something for him was normal. Would that have helped you, to have me confirm that what you felt was fine, and not a dirty, dysfunctional secret? Maybe then you wouldn't have done this. It just never occurred to me to do so. With the Neg-Vacs, you don't consider things like that yourself, not consciously, so applying it to other people doesn't come up, I guess?

⁵⁴ And as far as I'm concerned it's an ugly, involuntary action. Still, you felt the same about how you sometimes scratch behind your ear when you're nervous. It's liking little things about your partner, even if they don't like them, that adds to the love.

⁵⁵ This and the mention of false positives. You're trying to convince yourself that you would have acted before now if the feelings were real. Is that something you questioned yourself with before you did it? Or is it a thought line that stopped you going further than I saw? If you did stop.

⁵⁶ My friend said the systems in place in this instance are morals, both internal and externally promoted. There used to be a lot more variance between the two in some ways. We may still see bigotry, but it's a dying trait. Or so the Government tells us. Eventually, Neg-Vacs will cure us of all hate. Even this would be seen as a positive, apparently. It has helped identify an issue and given a way to deal with it. I still feel like I'm misusing it though.

The docking process had gone far more smoothly than Josh expected. The Orca linked up with Ailuros Unit Twenty-Three without issue and, though it took some time, they had gotten it out of its free roll without any real issues. But of course, something was bound to screw it all up. So, he rechecked the scans of the unit for the third time.

Alice shook her head. "This can't be right. The report said that the unit was cut loose with enough power and oxygen for six months. According to scans though, almost everything is still operational."[53]

Josh glanced up in time to see Alex wrinkle their nose at the statement, just like they always did when they were in deep thought. As far as he was concerned it was adorable.[54]

"Is there any indication as to why?" Alex asked. "I know that these systems allow some leeway when it comes to estimates, but an extra two years and still showing pretty good levels seems a bit much."

"Don't be dense," Lucy replied, her voice a mixture of derision and frustration. "This was a biological incident. That means a viral outbreak. Oxygen output would have been set to the average consumption level for whatever time measurement they used for scan intervals. The unit probably just picked up on the drop in usage when people started dying off and reduced the output of everything in line with that."

"Except it's still pumping out small amounts now," Josh said, glancing up at Lucy. "And showing life signs."

Lucy shrugged. "Rats. Or false positives."

"What makes you say that?" Alice asked.

"If they've got power, they've got comms. If there was anyone still alive, they'd have called for help by now.[55] Plus, the unit was in free roll, right?"

"Ye-es," Alice replied, drawing the word out as she went over the scans again.

"Well, these units aren't built to just allow that." Lucy turned to Stuart and continued, "You. You used to work on Ailuros. They're built with self-righting systems to stop the units rolling while hooked up, and in case of accidental ejection, right?"

He nodded. "They are, yeah."[56]

"Because nobody likes to fuck with the room spinning around them. Given

[57] Your split with him wasn't caused by a single, sharp blow. It was a sustained blast of issues that left a mark you can paint over but can't just hammer out.

[58] There's still a part of you that would save the relationship with him if you could. Even now. That's another thing that hurts.

[59] You still felt more for him than you realized. That makes sense to me as an interpretation here. It could be my anger, trying to make it worse. It could also be me trying to protect myself though; if there's love there, that's more understandable than if it's just plain temptation. Being cheated on for love makes sense, the other person meaning nothing leaves you asking, 'How little do I mean then?'

the apparent power levels in there, if there were survivors, they'd have kicked the thrusters in and righted themselves. I bet there's signs of damage on the exterior."

"Hang on," Alice said, and pulled up an external scan. "There's some potential cosmetic damage one side. It doesn't look like a blunt impact, it's more of a burn, so I doubt it was debris."[57]

Lucy shrugged. "So maybe it was an external explosion. The point is, any damage is a sign of some sort of force on one side. That would push it into a roll, and any survivors would have righted that."

Josh crossed his arms. As much as he was loathe to admit it, there was a good chance that Lucy was right. Still, preparing for the worst was always the safer bet. "And if you're wrong, and there are still people alive in there?"

Aaron let out a loud snort and replied, "Then we salvage some lives along with the tech."[58]

"It may not be that simple," Rob added. "What if there are survivors but the virus is still active?"

Alice called up a holographic projection of the medical scans. "No, I think we're safe on that front. Nothing is coming up on our external scans or the linked up internal scans. There are no known or unknown viral signals on board."

"So, maybe some people were immune, and the comms weren't working?" Kevin tried. "They could have gotten broken during any panic, right?"

Alex looked to Stuart and asked, "Any chance that could be right?"

Stuart scratched his head through the projection of short, blonde bangs. "I mean, I worked in a different unit, but they were pretty much all set up the same. The communication system mostly just ran internally, through the unit and to the central hub. They had an external emergency broadcast, but you needed a code to activate it."

"So, if the wrong people died, it could be that anyone still alive has been stuck there with no way to call out?"

"In theory. But there were failsafes. The code was allocated digitally and would automatically pass to the three most senior staff members that the scans pick up as still living. If all the staff died, then the guests were ranked in order of likely usefulness in an emergency. Someone would have had access."

Alex turned back towards Alice and Josh. "How many life signs are we getting?"

"A lot," Josh replied. "More than there should be for this low a level of oxygen use."[59]

[60] Did he push for you to sleep with him, I wonder? Is that what this is? You could be strong, but you had limits, and he broke them. We all have limits, Josh. But it wasn't a gunfight. You simply had to step out of the line of fire. That you didn't means part of you wanted it.

[61] I feel a little insulted. Worse is knowing that it's probably an accurate reaction. Certainly publicly, I never did shout you down or take a firm approach. Maybe that makes me a bad person, letting conflict play out behind closed doors rather than going public like you were used to. I don't know. I don't think either of us were intentionally terrible in that regard. Couples argue sometimes. Still. Maybe this is a sign that you needed me to find ways to talk you down sometimes rather than dancing around it. What you did, even if it didn't go as far as I think it did, was shitty. But I'm clearly not blameless in where we've gotten to.

Lucy let out a loud groan. "I'm telling you, it's false positives. Whatever happened in there, people panicked, things got broken. End of."

Alex nodded. "Still. If there is anyone still there, they've potentially been alone for a long time. We may need to bring something for protection. Just in case. Stuart, what did security use when you worked there?"

"Shock gloves, mostly. No firearms. The walls are safe, but…" he trailed off.

"But not dense enough to withstand projectiles.[60] Okay. Alice, can you bring the oxygen output up to a breathable level remotely?"

"Sure," she replied and started tapping through screens. "Give me twenty minutes or so, and it should be fine. I'll get the lights up as well. It looks like at least a few of the security cameras on board are working, but aren't recording, so we're gonna be relying on real time scans to keep track of each other. Everyone is carrying Mag Boots, right?"

Alice waited, and when no negative response came, continued, "Some of those rooms are supposed to be pretty tall. Looking at the power readings, we should be able to use the Mag Boots on a contactless charge setting without any issues if we need to get down quickly. Or if we need to dislodge something tight."

Alex smiled. "Okay, Good. Aaron, can you head to storage and see what weapons we have available non-firearm wise?"

"And why would I want to do that?" Aaron asked, puffing his chest out again.

"For fuck's sake," Josh grumbled. "How about, because…"

Alex raised a hand and gave Josh a pleading look. Josh frowned, confused by Alex's reaction, but let them run with it.

"You will do it because the Guild Director appointed Josh and me as leads for this salvage," Alex stated, their voice calm and measured. "Now, if you have something useful to add, I am happy to listen. But know this. I am equally as happy to report refusals of reasonable requests to Miss Walker. I wouldn't want to see your percentage cut."

For a moment, the room was silent as the shock of Alex standing up to Aaron sunk in.[61]

Then, a dark cackle broke it, drawing everyone's attention to Lucy. "Looks like the posh princess has grown a pair. Come on, Colt. I'll give you a hand."

Though visibly fuming, Aaron followed Lucy's command and they both left the room.

Rob floated over to Alex and gave them a pat on the back. "Well done."

FILE NAME: EXPLORATORY INTERVIEW (IV)
FILE REFERENCE: 4375405350687895994100356550225
TRANSCRIBED BY: ██████ ███ , ████ ████

MARK TYLER: For the purposes of clarity, I would like to note that Sarah Walker requested a break at this point in the recordings. Are you okay?

SARAH WALKER: Yeah. Sorry. It's just strange thinking that this is the last footage of the entire crew alive on board The Orca.

MARK TYLER: The last footage of anyone is…strange to review. I'm afraid this won't get any easier.

SARAH WALKER: No. No, I'm sure it won't. And you can't confirm who is still alive? Or how people died?

MARK TYLER: Unfortunately, no. The company places some importance on the need to see raw reactions. Supplying more information than we have would—

SARAH WALKER: [Interrupting, frustrated] Potentially allow me to formulate a response in advance. In other words, make excuses. [Sighs] I'm sorry, I don't mean to take it out on you specifically. I understand the rules, I have to use a cold structure myself at times, but it doesn't mean I like it.

MARK TYLER: Well, let's talk a little about what we've just watched. Was Lucy Foster's assertion that life scans were either false positives or rats the correct one?

SARAH WALKER: It's a typical Lucy answer. She takes a very straight forward approach to salvages. If there's an obvious answer, as far as she's concerned, it's the correct answer.

MARK TYLER: Would you have come to the same conclusion if you were in her shoes?

SARAH WALKER: Without seeing the scans, I couldn't say. I tended to read things thoroughly before suggesting things like that.

MARK TYLER: But based on what you know from the video?

SARAH WALKER: Standard procedure in a joint salvage is to have at least two people review scans before feeding back to the other crew members. That way, what one person misses, another might catch. Alice and Josh are pretty thorough so the fact that neither of them mentioned any specific abnormalities to specifically indicate another option, and taking into account the timeframe between ejection and salvaging... I'd say that I most likely would have, yes.

MARK TYLER: So, was it wrong to explore the possibility of survivors? Was that perhaps a way to undermine Lucy Foster? Maybe to, I don't know, pay her and Aaron Colt back for their attitudes?

SARAH WALKER: No, I don't think so. While rats or false positives seems more likely, given the ejection related to a biological incident, I'd say they were just playing it safe.

MARK TYLER: Are you certain? There did seem to be a united front to shoot the idea down.

SARAH WALKER: You're wrong. None of them said the words 'you are wrong,' they just offered alternatives. They asked, 'what if.' If nothing else, Rob would have told her outright if he thought she was wrong.

MARK TYLER: Oh? What makes you say that?

SARAH WALKER: You saw how he dealt with Colt. Plus, we had that date.

MARK TYLER: [Smiles] Fair enough. Was Alex's decision correct?

SARAH WALKER: Absolutely. Alex was planning for the most problematic potential. It wouldn't cause issues if Lucy turned out to be right but would mean they were prepared if she wasn't.

MARK TYLER: Okay, good. Can I ask you something a little off topic?

SARAH WALKER: [Waves her hand in the positive]

MARK TYLER: Guild Directors don't tend to do salvages themselves unless it's an emergency. At forty-seven, you're pretty young to be retired from active salvaging. Do you miss it?

SARAH WALKER: [Smiles] Every day.

[62] That one is a direct quote. You're right, there are better paid—and easier—jobs than the one I do at the Funeral Home. It is kinda like a drug to me though. I don't know what it is about it. There's just something about being around a full blown vision of the life cycle that makes me feel like I need to be there. My boss felt the same. For him, it was because mourning had a different feel now that we have Neg-Vacs. He's old enough to remember the last 'free deaths' as he called them. Maybe that's it. Maybe it's therapeutic in a way.

[63] And which of us is keeping things in and not talking about them now? If this is literal, then you never mentioned how much my job bothered you.

[64] Again, if this is what it seems to be, then part of you feels like I'm not only to blame for what happened, but somehow caused it to happen. Intentionally. I can tell you that you're wrong on that. Perhaps I could have acted on certain signs, but I never intentionally let us fall into this pit. I wanted us to work.

MARK TYLER: My husband once told me that the job is like a drug. For career salvagers, at least. I asked him why he did it once. He was qualified to do much easier jobs. Do you know what he said?

SARAH WALKER: That he felt like he *had* to do it.[62]

MARK TYLER: Exactly that.

SARAH WALKER: I don't know whether it's the adrenaline of the inherent danger, the physicality of it, or the regular space travel. For those of us that hear it calling, we *have* to answer. If you don't feel like you have to, you shouldn't be in the business.

MARK TYLER: That makes it harder, in a way. I was there when he started out, and I encouraged him. I wonder when he stopped standing at the cliff edge and dove off into the forever? Perhaps I could have convinced him to do something else with his life.

SARAH WALKER: Would you have wanted to *not* support him.

MARK TYLER: [Shakes head] No. No, I wouldn't have.[63]

SARAH WALKER: Can I ask another question?

MARK TYLER: Go ahead.

SARAH WALKER: You said that your husband entered the unit, but when my team got there, it was in free roll. Lucy was right that they aren't designed to just let that happen, and Alice found the burn mark on the outside. Your husband died, didn't he? And not in the unit. He was outside. His ship—

MARK TYLER: [Cuts in] Exploded, yes. Intentionally, judging by the last black box recording.[64]

SARAH WALKER: What the hell is in that unit? [Shakes her head] I'm sorry. For bringing it up. And for your loss.

MARK TYLER: Thank you. Shall we continue?

SARAH WALKER: [Takes a deep breath and exhales] Okay. Yes.

[65] <The concept at play here is using micromovements to control actions while synched up with a larger system. Stuart has issues at first but gets them moving. I believe this is a subtle acknowledgement that the subject knows what they are supposed—and perhaps, want—to do, but feel that they achieve it slowly rather than when they should.>

[66] Working on the basis that the unit is a cage for your actions apparently means that there's an appeal in falling for you. Microgravity isn't technically floating you see, it's a constant free fall. I suppose you did tend to put yourself in difficult positions. I read once that people can get addicted to failure. It seems like such a big part of their life that it becomes the norm. Nobody likes stepping outside their comfort zone. It's sad that we work that way sometimes.

FILE NAME: RECORDING EIGHT – THE ORCA, SYNCHED AUDIO LOGS
FILE REFERENCE: 437599211409040099516366464897
TRANSCRIBED BY: ▆▆ ▆▆ – ▆▆▆

The crew filed into the Ailuros unit's hanger and, once the doors had slid shut, Alice began testing her Mag Boots. With a tap on her Wrist Display, they locked her in place on the ground. Satisfied, she adjusted the settings and tried walking a few steps. The pressure sensitive pads lining the inside of her boots were clearly sending signals to the unit's system, telling it to adjust the magnetization level, but it was a little slow to respond.

"Is anyone having trouble getting their boots to adjust to movement?" she asked.

"Mine are a little slow…" Stuart began. "Nevermind, sorted.[65] Microgravity has always been the selling point of Ailuros.[66] We hardly ever used this setting unless we needed to work on ground level parts, so the units aren't the most up to date with micromovement measurement software."

Aaron let out an exaggerated sigh, making sure it was loud enough for everyone to hear. "Well, ain't that great. It's not gonna stick us in place, is it?"

Stuart shrugged. "It shouldn't."

"Quit complaining," Alex cut in. "If you get stuck, just shut it off and reboot the suit manually."

"Fucking prick," Aaron grunted.

"Ignore him," Lucy whispered. "Come on."

Josh stepped to the front of the group and said, "Standard protocol says we split into groups for the initial run through. Looking at the power levels, we may as well take our time over this. So, who wants to work the terminal to see if there's anything worth noting?"

"I'll do that," Alice replied, smiling widely. "I'd like to run a few of the in-built diagnostics, just to be sure that we have as much time as we think we do."

Alex nodded. "Stuart, you should probably stick there too. The system will be fairly familiar to you, right?"

"Only to a point, but sure."

Alice ran through the main menu and booted up the secure connection with the crew's Wrist Displays. "Map incoming."

Rob laughed. "That was quick."

Alice continued to work through the screens, focusing on learning the basic structure. "Simple systems I can work with."

"And you say you wouldn't be able to pilot," he replied.

[67] <This is not an uncommon piece of imagery these days, especially when dealing with trauma. Usually presented by the Superego, as it is here, it's basically a way of saying that it's trying to balance out the desires of the Id and Ego, but that sometimes, some things are just too old to be compatible with new ways of thinking. That, in itself, is a bad sign when it comes to changing behaviours.>

[68] <This on the other hand is a sign of hope. The Orca is being used as a means to get the necessary information out of the pseudo cage. It's essentially being set up as a way to transport understanding. If this related to an actual crime rather than infidelity, the absence of this line, you would have sacrificed any chance of rehabilitation based purely on the point about lack of compatibility. The subject would have been deemed a risk. Given that such thinking is usually overriding, I highly recommend that the subject doesn't commit any crimes.>

[69] <Inner turmoil. The subject feels like their natural impulses are sabotaging them, and their inability to control them makes them angry.>

"I said simple systems, not potential space coffins."

Kevin floated over and stood next to Stuart. "Does this look like the unit you worked on?" he asked.

Stuart called the map up as a holographic projection and rotated it, taking in the basic layout. "The layout is almost identical."

Alex smiled. "Okay, good. That means if we get lost, you're our Sat Nav. Hey, Alice, you said the cameras are working but not recording. Is there any chance you could synch them with our communicators?"

Kevin floated over and stood next to Stuart. "Does this look like the unit you worked on?" he asked.

Stuart called the map up as a holographic projection and rotated it, taking in the basic layout. "The layout is almost identical."

Alex smiled. "Okay, good. That means if we get lost, you're our Sat Nav. Hey, Alice, you said the cameras are working but not recording. Is there any chance you could synch them with our communicators?"

Alice swiped through the error report on the screen and tried again to get the system talking to her Wrist Display. "Way ahead of you. No go though. The system is too old. It's just not compatible.[67] The Orca has some compatibility options though.[68] I've already got it recording what's happening. We can't watch in real time, but we are live."

"That's great. Now," Alex replied. They turned to face the rest of the crew and frowned. "Where are Aaron and Lucy?"

Josh tapped the comms button on his Wrist Display. "Colt. Where did you and Foster get to?"

"We're doing our initial run-through," he replied through the communicator, his voice dripping with mock innocence. "Thanks for the map by the way, it says we're on the staff access-only side."

"Great. That's great. And what if we run into someone down here? You two have the only Shock Gloves."

"Oh, yeah. Sorry about that. Guess we'll have to share when we get back."

Aaron cut the communication and Josh raised his arms in frustration.

Alex drifted over and gave Josh a quick hug. "Ignore them, Puss-Puss. They're trying to get you angry."

"They're doing a good job of it,"[69] Josh sighed. "Alright. I'm gonna check out the retail section. Rob, do you fancy joining me?"

"Sure."

Alex flipped their map back on and giggled. "I think I've spotted what you have. Fingers crossed it's working. Okay, that leaves me and Kevin with the

[70] Given her core duty of keeping the other facets in check, I suppose she technically does work on the systems side of things.

[71] <Alice took her role because Rob couldn't and is moving forward with other projects. She was also the first to kickback at Aaron in the hangar, entirely to stop him derailing things. That would make her the Ideal Self part of the duo. She behaves how you would expect someone to, stands for what's right, and has career aspirations. That means Rob is the conscience, hence he stepped in second to support her push against Aaron.>

[72] <Stuart has a good understanding of the unit, at least to a point. He is actively suggesting ways forward, even though he openly doesn't know how easy it would be to do what needs to be done. He may be a representation of the subject's past mistakes. Or to be more precise, hope to move beyond them.>

living quarters and lower deck medical area. Are you okay with that?"

"Of course," Kevin replied.

"Excellent. In that case, let's get to it."

Alice called up the real time monitoring system on the terminal screen and watched the blips representing the two pairs as they pushed off the floor bars and made their way to the only door to the main unit. There, they split off in different directions. It seemed fairly accurate. The real trick would be getting them to synch up with the Wrist Displays.

Stuart leaned over and watched her swipe through screens. "So do you work a lot with the systems side of things?"[70]

"I tinker. Honestly, it's mostly just because Rob can't handle anything other than click-and-it-works.[71] The moment something goes wrong, he gives up. Piloting is the only thing that doesn't apply to. The electronics side can be fun too though. I've been working on some small custom routines for Skin Suits for example. You know how Director Walker's jacket moves? That was me. The standard projection looked too stiff to me, so I edited it."

"Really? That's cool."

Alice smiled at his delight and added a cool, "Yup."

Stuart pointed at a window at the side of the screen. "The diagnostics look clear."

"They do. I'm struggling to get the life sign scanner linked up to our displays though. Would that normally be done in these units?"

Stuart nodded. "Only for staff. If we run through the list of people on board, we may be able to find the allocated security code. We could probably get it to register our displays as temporary residents and access the whole system then."

Alice stopped typing and glanced over at Stuart. "Wouldn't the code be out of commission now? If everyone is dead, I mean."

"No. It would still be allocated to the last person alive. That may let us know if the system at least thinks that everyone is dead too."

Alice flexed her fingers. "Which would lend some credence to Foster's rat idea. Okay, let's take a detour, Mr. Terminal. Think it'll be easy?"

"No idea. The security system at my unit was pretty robust."[72]

Alice smiled. "That's fine. I like a challenge."

[73] This fits the narrative, I suppose, but in reality, I do have some minor medical knowledge. Only when it comes to the treatment of dead bodies mind you, but it's there. That's down to me, not my parents though.

[74] <The subject appears to have a need for duality in his Waking Dream. Aaron and Lucy are the Id and Ego, which are commonly paired up. Josh and Alex are obviously representations of the subject and his partner (though potentially not literally, it may be that Alex for example is more of a representation of how he sees them in relation to his life). Rob and Alice represent both sides of the Superego. Mark and Sarah are the duo tasked with making sense of things. Stuart and Kevin meanwhile, are his attempt to fix past mistakes. Stuart is moving forward, and Kevin is seeking to simply understand them.>

Duality makes sense. Do you remember what you said to me when I asked what you fear the most? You said, 'being alone.' You aren't built to be on your own. You need to be in a pair. 'That's why I keep trying,' you said. I know you felt like it was selfish to feel that way, but honestly, Josh, most of us are like that. We're a social species, and the more we struggle, the more we feel the need for the comfort of others. So don't feel bad about wanting to be with someone.

Alex snatched a tablet out of the air and turned it over in their hand, checking the make and model. They batted a free-floating pillow to the side and noted the item on the shared salvage list on their Wrist Display.

"Looks like some of the locks and magnets are failing," they said. "Note everything you spot, even if it's small and not worth much. Ships the size of The Orca have a good amount of storage boxes, but it's still worth knowing exactly how much space we need."

Kevin grabbed a watch and replied, "And we want to be able to prioritize the items, right? Like, if we can only carry so much, we need to know what's where and what's more worth taking."

"Exactly. You'd be surprised what personal experience can do, too. When we compare the lists before getting the storage boxes on board, it may be that something you or I think is low value may actually be high value. Case in point, when we hit the medical bay, most people won't know what they're looking at with the drugs on board. You often find salvagers either taking it all or leaving it all. Me, I've got a good idea which ones will be worth more in resale."

"Is that something you picked up working with your Dad? He's in pharmaceuticals, isn't he?"[73]

Alex smiled. "You've been researching."

"I like to know who I'm working with.[74] I only asked around a little though."

"I bet the answers you got weren't entirely positive."

"...No." Kevin paused, then asked, "Is it true that you don't really need to be here? Because you run two companies?"

Alex gave a short, gentle laugh and turned to look at Kevin. "I thought that may be coming. No, though, it's not. I'm listed as a director, yes, because my father needed the positions filled. He runs it all though, and I only step in when I'm absolutely needed. Salvaging is my only steady income."

"So your Dad doesn't even pay you?" Kevin grimaced. "That's cruel."

"Not really. Have you ever met a genuinely rich person?" Kevin shook his head and Alex continued, "If you trace it back far enough, rich families all had a point where they weren't rich. The problem is, when they've lived with money for a long enough time, some forget that and start to think that they're above everyone else. They appreciate others who were born into money like they

[75] This was sad to read, Josh. The talk of money is probably borne from your dislike of those in power, but the social standing thing is the important bit. I know my friends weren't fair to you, even when you hauled yourself out of your more destructive habits. I also know that your old friends turned on you when you weren't a wild, party animal anymore. I had no idea that it left you feeling this hopeless. I'm sorry I never noticed.

<As a side note on this, money rarely represents money in dreams, so to apply it to something else here is correct. The usual interpretation is 'self-worth' but given the nature of this scenario and the need for personal knowledge of the subject, it may well be that a dislike for those in power is correct here.>

[76] You're making this hard. Not intentionally, because you had no idea I was doing this. But seeing that expressed by part of you, even if it's a loose representation of me as part of you hammers home that I do matter. That makes it harder to think that I may walk away from you. It also makes it harder to understand why you did what you did.

were because they're the same. If someone finds a way to come into money though? They're interlopers."

Alex signalled for them to move on, and the pair made their way to the next unlocked room while they continued their story. "My family wasn't poor, but we didn't have more than we needed. Then, my father got lucky. A couple of good business decisions, and he was able to open his own companies and build a portfolio of decent clients. Things were fine for a little while, but soon enough, the nastier end of the born-rich crowd realized where we came from."

"What did they do?"

"They sabotaged my father's business deals. They upped prices for important stocks and made competing offers for clients, even if it meant making a loss themselves. That was the point though. They could lose some sales and cut deals that left them short, and their bank accounts would just swallow it. They wanted us to know that. My family though? Each loss made a difference."

Kevin paused again, thinking it through. "You're in debt, aren't you?"

"Me, personally? No. My father made sure that all debt fell on him. His businesses are failing though. I hold my roles to support him, and work salvages to feed myself."

"Huh. So you improved your social standing and that made the people you rose to meet hate you. Then you fell back down and the people on the level you started at rejected you because you'd been higher. Makes you wonder why any of us bother to try improving our lives."[75]

Alex shrugged and started tilting a portable video screen that was still locked down. "I don't anymore. Not because of that though."

"Then why?"

"Because I met Josh. Whether we're excelling or just surviving makes no difference. We're still together. If we have that, life is more than good enough."[76]

Alex, having said their peace, let the silence sit comfortably while they continued to work, moving from room to room.

Eventually, Kevin frowned and said, "That's…strange."

"What is?"

"This is the fifth room we've looked at. I know the first two had been cleaned out, but, it's just…why haven't we come across any bodies yet? If everyone, or even most people, died, shouldn't we have seen something by now?"

Alex crossed their arms. "Hmm…well, let's assume it was a viral outbreak. Maybe the crew attempted to stem the spread. If someone died, it's possible

[77] Of course they do in my line of work.

[78] True. Children and animals are the hardest to deal with. It's an unfortunate part of the job. I've learned to shut it out, but it's still not nice.

[79] Also true, I guess? For those of us viewing this from the outside, we don't' really know what happened. And with how much you're struggling to understand things, you don't really know all of it either, do you? Maybe this will be good for both of us in that regard.

that they…well…got rid of the body."

"Like…shot it into space?"

"Exactly. You find bodies floating once in a while. Chances are, even if they shot a few out at a time, they'd all be picked up by different people and nobody would be any the wiser. Or, they could have burned them."

Alex continued to work, but noticed Kevin floating in place, watching them. "You okay?" they asked.

Kevin ran his hand over his head, his fingers disappearing inside the designer scruff of his hair projection. "You're very calm about that. Body disposal, I mean."

"When you've done this long enough, bodies become almost common place.[77] Most derelicts have at least one."

Kevin shivered. "I'm not sure I want to reach a point where death doesn't upset me."

"I never said it didn't upset me. Children and animals. They really get me.[78] This place had a no pets rule and was over eighteens only, so both should be ruled out."

Kevin floated over and helped Alex move the nearby bed, freeing a small satchel. "What about Foster's rat idea?"

"If there are rats," Alex replied, carefully skimming over the jewellery in the bag, "they would have had to have snuck in with a supply shipment. Pets I find more upsetting than sneaky food raiders. I think the false positives idea is more likely anyway though. Plus, you have to remember one thing."

"What's that?"

"Nobody living knows what happened here. Right now, all we have is guesswork."[79]

[80] <This was likely Lucy's idea. Both the Id and Ego seek pleasure, and the Ego tries to find ways to achieve it without risking negative consequences. It has no sense of right or wrong, but views something as good if it achieves it goal without harming either itself or the Id. Here, they've messed with the other crew members in a way that would not be found out in time to result in any major consequences.>

FILE NAME: EXPLORATORY INTERVIEW (V)
FILE REFERENCE: 4375284061220519190512603029771
TRANSCRIBED BY: ███ ███

MARK TYLER: I wanted to stop for a moment here as the next file is…it's likely to be a focus for you, and I wanted to ask a few quick questions first.

SARAH WALKER: Actually, I have one too.

MARK TYLER: Go ahead.

SARAH WALKER: How many Shock Gloves were Aaron Colt and Lucy Foster carrying?

MARK TYLER: You will see that in a later clip, but one each.

SARAH WALKER: Would I be correct in assuming that they told the others that that's all that was on board?

MARK TYLER: Uhm, I'd need to check that. I would think that's a safe bet though, given nobody brought it up.[80] Why is that?

SARAH WALKER: Because I checked the on board stock levels myself. There were enough Shock Gloves on board for a ten-person crew to be fully armed, plus a handful of rifles.

MARK TYLER: Rifles?

SARAH WALKER: Yes. Don't worry, they all fit within the insurance and shared usage contracts. You can check that yourselves, I'm sure.

MARK TYLER: Why do you think they would lie about that?

SARAH WALKER: In that instance, they were messing with their crewmates, I'm sure. I'm glad they didn't break the no firearms ruling, but that was reckless.

MARK TYLER: A sign that they were certain that there were no survivors, perhaps?

SARAH WALKER: Even if it was, that's enough to lead to a disciplinary. Anyway. You had questions?

[81] This one is on you. You know that you didn't tell me everything. Or anything in this case.

[82] I suppose I did that a few times, didn't I? I actually felt kinda guilty about that. Joking about death isn't really right. It was a coping mechanism to a point though. I only ever joked when things were tough. Does that justify doing it?

MARK TYLER: Yes. Sticking with Colt and Foster, should they have wandered off like they did?

SARAH WALKER: Given the situation, no. Technically speaking they are fine to work as a pair, and they're allowed to take whatever section they want unless the salvage leads say otherwise. Protocol says the crew stays together until ordered to do the run-through, though. It allows them to keep track of each other and know where everyone else is expected to be. I will say though, this is a minor issue compared to the weaponry.

MARK TYLER: Alice seems to be quite useful to have around.

SARAH WALKER: When it comes to getting things online, absolutely. She's not the most qualified in the Guild, but she's definitely effective. It's the age-old tale of a lack of official papers not equalling a lack of actual skills.

MARK TYLER: [Smiles] Are you making the qualification point to prove that you weren't unduly influenced in your decision to send her on the salvage?

SARAH WALKER: [Chuckles] Yes. Yes, I am.

MARK TYLER: There's no need. Honestly. My question was whether she was likely to be able to spot if files stored on the unit's servers had been modified or deleted.

SARAH WALKER: Hmm. I don't know. If she was looking for evidence of that, maybe? Does this relate to what you said about Ailuros withholding information?[81]

MARK TYLER: Maybe. Anyway, moving on to what Alex said, are bodies really that common?

SARAH WALKER: Yes. When you visit enough derelicts, you realize that not everything is abandoned. But sometimes, people are.

MARK TYLER: We're a strange species sometimes. From a personal standpoint, my husband rarely talked about that side of things, and when he did, he tended to make a joke of it.[82] Do all salvagers grow to expect it, or is it more of a 'each person finds their own way to cope' kinda thing?

[83] You never needed to, Josh. You were there if I felt the need to talk, and that was all you needed to do. Maybe I should have made that clear.

SARAH WALKER: It's a bit of both, I think. Joking about it isn't uncommon.

MARK TYLER: It's odd to think about it, at least when you're on the outside looking in. It must be hard to shoulder, though. I wish I'd been better at giving him an outlet.[83] [Coughs] Okay. The next clip is going to be tough. After you see it though, you'll understand why this investigation is taking place.

[84] There's that duality again. Oh, and I knew it! You always said you wouldn't have tattoos or scarification, but you were also far too interested in it to not want it on some level. This proves it.

[85] That would actually look really good on you. Are you sure you're not a secret furry? For the record, it's fine if you are. Fursuits are adorable.

"Oh, cool, it's a SkAr," Josh exclaimed as he led Rob into the body mod parlour on the East side of the ground floor. He'd used the chain before, and always thought that the name was pretty clever. It was a dual reference; a portmanteau of 'Skin' and 'Art', but also a reference to scarification service they also offered.[84]

Josh glanced around the room and didn't even try to keep the smile form his face when he saw what he was looking for.

"Ah, there it is!" he said, and floated over to a large table in the middle of the room. He started powering up the attached screen. "And it's working! Now, let's see…"

Rob rolled his eyes. "A tattoo table? Really?"

"Yeah. I get some new ink every time we find a working one. Here we go."

Josh powered down the clothing projection on his Skin Suit and rolled the top part down to his waist. He positioned himself over the table, face down, and placed his hands and feet into the relevant slots. This caused a series of metal straps to slide out, locking him in place, but avoiding the Wrist Display. A second set of straps then slid out over his shoulders and upper thighs.

With a loud *thunk*, a long arm folded out from under the head of the table and started projecting a green light from its tip, scanning Josh's body.

"In places like this, a lot of the tools are automated," Josh explained. "You wouldn't be allowed near them without paying, but with the place being abandoned, there's no need."

The large arm retracted, and a series of smaller arms slid out from the sides, wriggling like an upturned beetle. After a few seconds, they closed in and started moving over Josh's body, the tattoo machines at their tips working on the pattern.

Josh let out a satisfied groan, embracing the initial surge of pain. When he looked up, he saw Rob studying him, no doubt taking in the leopard style patterning following the curves of his body.[85]

"Huh. So that's why Alex called you Puss-Puss."

"That's right. The machine is just extending the pattern this time, getting a little more coverage. When I'm happy with the skin art, I'll start looking at eye mods. Or maybe one of those tail implants they're working on in Tokyo. I already have the teeth, see?" Josh pulled his lips back to reveal small, feline fangs.

[86] I remember you saying something similar when we were talking about why you didn't like the Neg-Vac/Alleviation Sim system. You felt like everything was forced into line and you wanted to experience things yourself. Fully and wholly. Just as you. And, boy, did you do that when you were with him, from what you said. Maybe that plays into the of addiction of falling? I need to work with death, and you need to feel pain. Otherwise neither of us feel alive.

[87] Okay, not to stoke the flames of paranoia here, but that line is programmed, apparently. My friend said it's worked into every Alleviation Sim. You never remember it, but it creates an internal loop. The hair projections synch up with the concept of Neg-Vacs for some reason, and that makes you more willing to accept them. That has to do some damage for people like you who can't use them. You hate the concept but something is worked into the mandated Sims to make you want them to a degree. That should really be reviewed by those in charge.

Rob crossed his arms. "Well, that's…something. Why not just make use of the Skin Suits though? That was the whole point of the UN making them the only manufactured clothing, wasn't it? So you could download projections to make yourself look however you wanted?"Josh groaned and instinctively pushed into the needle. "I'm a tactile person. Skin suits are convenient for clothing, but when it comes to my body, I prefer to have something permanent that I can see and feel. Something that's just mine."[86]

"But you just picked the design from the standard list. Anyone could choose the same one, right?"

"Yes, but it won't sit on their skin the same way it does on mine. Skin suit projections look identical no matter who you are; this looks unique, even if it's only in a minor way."

Rob shrugged. "Fair enough. Is that why you don't have a hood on your Skin Suit too? To keep with your natural hair?"

"Yeah. It kinda sucks that we aren't allowed real haircuts these days. I mean, I get it.[87] The intelligent spores that got brought back with that first, what did they call it? A UN sanctioned Goldilocks Zone Planetary Exploration? They spread like crazy, right? And we technically still have them, at least when hair gets beyond a quarter inch in length.

"Like I said though, I'm tactile. I need something real, something I can feel. So, I stick with my natural head stubble. It's my way of saying I hate the regulation clothing mandate without breaking it. Minor rebellions get you in less trouble, right? Especially if nobody knows that's what you're doing. Did you tell Alex how to deal with Colt, by the way?"

Rob nodded and Josh continued, "Well, thank you for that. I'm more likely to fight fire with ten times more fire. If anyone can get Alex to deal with idiots in a way that doesn't leave me wanting to hit someone, I'm grateful."

"No problem. Honestly, I'm surprised Colt and Foster are still licensed with the way they behave."

"It's a perk of being good at your job."

"I guess so."

Rob's Wrist Display flashed, and he looked down at the screen. "Looks like Alice is synching us up with the internal scanners. That could be useful. Oh, she says they may not all synch up correctly though. Something to do with the scanners not being certain what they're looking at? Still, that's better than nothing."

"It might clear itself up as we go. It could just be that we've all caused a big change in what it's seeing and it's trying to figure out."

[88] I'm lucky in that regard. I haven't suffered so much that misgendering affects me. So, I can take intent into account. Not everyone can, though.

[89] This could be nothing, or it could be a nod towards masking. We all do that to a degree, and you're probably right that it doesn't quite work as intended. If someone knows you well enough, you know when something is up. Unfortunately, we don't always act on that knowledge. I guess I get as scared as you do sometimes.

"Maybe. So, you and Alex are together, right?"

Josh tensed up at the question, and let it seep into his response. "We are."

"No, no, it's nothing bad," Rob said, noticing his tone. "It's just, I was wondering something, and if you're together, you'd probably know better than if you just sometimes worked together."

Josh relaxed a little and replied, "What did you want to know?"

"I was just wondering if Alex had preferred pronouns? When you landed at HQ, Alex looked male. Slightly androgynous, but male. By the time we boarded The Orca though, there was..." He trailed off and waived his hands up and down his chest and waist.

"A chest and hips. Alex is genderfluid, so you'll see changes like that from time to time. As to pronouns, they/them is preferable, but Alex isn't the sort to get too worked up if you mess up, as long as it's not intentional."[88]

"Okay, good. The, uhm, padding looked like it was moving quite naturally. Was that a new skin suit projection routine?"

"No. Despite what people think, Alex is as almost broke as the rest of us. Our Skin Suits are actually the only rich-kid things we own, and these were salvage finds on an old military ship. When we saw what they did, we asked Sarah if we could keep them, and she just took the estimated price—minus our profit cut—off our total earnings for the salvage.

"Alex's allows minor physical shaping. It's got something to do with compressing the liquid coolant in the middle layer. I think these models come with extra coolant as a standard anyway. They'd have to or the projection screens would heat up too much when they run the stealth mode."

"Stealth mode? That's incredible. What's it like?"

"You've not seen it? The screens have built-in cameras. Basically, they film what's in front of them and project it onto the opposite screen. So the wall behind you is shown on your front, and the one in front of you is shown on the back. It's not perfect; if you move too much it's easy to spot, but it's not like we're running military ops or anything, so I don't see that it matters much. I doubt they work as well as they were intended in practice, but I guess if someone isn't paying full attention, they'd hide you pretty well.[89] When I'm done on here, I'll show you if you like."

"Sure."

The needle hit a sore point and Josh breathed deeply. "So, what do you think about all of this?"

"What happened here, you mean? I don't know. I'll tell you one thing though. I've seen blood on the walls and a lot of damaged doors, but not one

single body yet. That's creeping me out a bit."

Josh nodded. "I noticed that, too. It's weird. There was supposed to be, what, eighty-four people here? We should have found someone by now."

"That's what I was—" Rob stopped mid-sentence and looked over at the open door at the far end of the room. "Did you hear that?"

"Hear what?""Hold on. I'm gonna check it out."

Rob pushed off the wall and moved out the door, leaving Josh still locked in place on the table.

"Check what out?" Josh asked, raising his voice. When no reply came, he tried again, but louder. "Rob?"

Josh's Wrist Display lit up and Rob's voice came through. "Sorry, I'm here. I just thought I heard…wait. That can't…oh, shit. Get back. Get…" Rob screamed. Then, he stopped.

The table still working, Josh was unable to reach his Wrist Display, so he resorted to yelling. "Rob? Hey, Rob! What's going on?"

Bang.

A heavy bang rang out, and Josh's head snapped around to meet it. It was coming from outside the wall that hid the hallway Rob had entered. Rhythmically, it starts to move slowly towards the door.

Bang.

Bang.

Bang.

Josh panicked and tried to force himself free, but the straps audibly tightened in response. "C'mon. Finish," he mumbled.

Bang.

The banging reached the edge of the door and stopped. Josh looked up at the empty door, breathing rapidly.

"Rargh!" Rob yelled, swinging through the door, with a huge smile on his face that only grew when he heard Josh's high-pitched scream.

The table let out a beep, and the tattoo machines at the tips of the table's arms flipped over, quickly applying a layer of antiseptic. The straps loosened, and Josh floated free, turning to face Rob as he angrily pulled his Skin Suit back up.

"You absolute bastard," he growled.

Rob laughed. "I'm so sorry. I just couldn't resist."

"Maybe you should have tried a bit harder."

Rob continued to laugh while Josh powered his clothing projection back on.

Josh shook his head and looked up, opening his mouth to say something,

[90] <Monsters are common symbols in dreams. In Carl Jung's work, they often played the role of the Shadow. This is a representation of the darker side of the psyche. It's like the Id, in a way. For a lot of people, the Id is based around the idea of going against societal norms though, while the Shadow is going against both that and personal morals. Here, it is the subject's guilt, and the way he views what happened.>

The scary thing is that it existing kinda proves that you did do something at least. The conscience brings about guilt for doing wrong. The guilt won here. That means your impulses were stronger than your conscience.

but the words caught in his throat. Everything happened too quickly. One moment, Rob was there, laughing. The next, *something* floated up behind him, lurched forward, and dragged him back into the hall.

Now Rob screamed again, but it was very different to the one he gave down the Wrist Display. It was full of pure, primal fear.

Then there was the crunching.

And the wet suction.

Then, Rob's cries became a choked cough, and disappeared entirely.

Josh pushed off the table, moving slowly towards the door. "Rob! What the fuck is…"

Josh grabbed a floor bar and stopped. Blood had started to float into view just beyond the doorway, the microgravity causing it to spread as though it was in water.[90]

Josh panicked.

He grabbed the floor bars and hauled himself backwards, colliding with the tattoo table as he tried to turn and head back to the door he and Rob had originally entered through.

His body working on nothing but an instinctual need to escape, he was back at the hangar before he knew it.

[91] <A desire to abort the simulation when faced with a hard truth. This is well documented as a common occurrence. That's the one drawback with the system, I think. Everything is repressed and we only get one Alleviation Sim each month. That means we get a build-up thrown at us in one go. That's why they ensure we don't remember much, if any, of the simulation after it ends. For the subject, who does not normally experience Neg-Vac use, this is particularly difficult here, as no part of their brain is used to the Alleviation Sim being this ramped up.>

I really screwed up, didn't I?

[92] <This ties in with the note about the monster. That moment was impulse defeating conscience. Now the Ideal Self is trying to right that by showing boundaries.>

Alice heard the rapid slap of hands on metal bars and turned from the terminal. It was Josh, his face etched with fear. She watched as he tapped his Wrist Display and yelled, "Get back to the hangar. We need to get out of here. Now!"

Alice looked down at her own Wrist Display, noticing that he'd sent the message to everyone. She frowned. "What's going on? Where's Rob?"

"We need to go!"[91] Josh repeated.

Alex and Kevin floated into the hangar and Alex immediately went to their partner, asking, "Josh, what happened?"

"He's dead," Josh replied, speaking quickly. "Rob is dead. We were in the body mod parlour. Something grabbed him. It was so quick, I—"

"Oh, real funny," Alice cut in. She tapped her Wrist Display and continued, "Seriously, Rob? This again?" When no response came, she grunted, "I'm going to go get him."

Josh reached out and grabbed her, yelling, "No! Don't!"

"Josh, calm down," Alex tried.

"You don't get it. We need to leave."

Alice yanked herself free and pushed off towards the main door. "Whatever. When I get Rob back here, we're going to have a nice chat about boundaries."[92]

She made her way through the hall with a look of rage on her face. Eventually, she spotted the sign for SkAr, and pulled herself in. "Not funny, Rob! I told you about this last time. Where are you, you..."

Alice's voice trailed off as her head turned towards the opposite doorway. There was blood floating gently in place. And a hand, cut off at the wrist. Alice looked froze in place, taking in what she was seeing. *A Wrist Display.*

Alice swallowed and lifted her hand, tapping Rob's name and hitting the comms button. "Rob? Hello?"

She heard her own voice pour out from the device on the floating hand, the slight delay created an echo effect.

"This can't be real," she whispered.

The fingers on the hand twitched.

Alice grabbed the floor bars and rushed back out to the hallways, pushing herself towards the hangar. The moment she made it inside, she grabbed Josh,

[93] <When the standards of your Ideal Self are too high, everything results in failure. This reaction is rooted in the narrative, but it is also a personal reaction from the subject.>

In other words, you know you failed to act the way you wanted, or felt you should, and you're panicking about facing that fact and what the consequences of it will be.

[94] The capital letters are an anagram for CHEAT. That's a pretty clear indicator that you know what the monster is.

[95] <This doesn't necessarily mean that the subject is no longer trying to understand the reasons behind his actions. It's more likely that, on some level, he accepts that the act itself exists, whether there is a deeper explanation or not.>

her eyes pleading as she asked, "What the hell happened? This is just a shitty joke, right?[93] You found some Halloween props and some red dye or something. Right?"

"He says that something attacked them," Alex said.

"Who?" Alice screamed. "Who attacked you? A survivor?"

Josh shook his head. "It wasn't human. We need to get back on The Orca and leave."

Stuart turned back to the terminal and said, "I'll get the inner door unlocked."

Alice barely registered a quiet, *Click. Click-click* heading towards the room but pushed the sound away as she tried again to find out what happened. "Please! What happened? What attacked you? Describe it."

"Hey, wait," Kevin said. "What about Foster and Col—"

Before Kevin could finish, a fast moving shape slammed into him, forcing him against the terminal. The impact knocked Stuart aside. It also causes the terminal to spark and explode.

The lights in the hangar started to flicker, leaving the crew barely able to see anything but flashes of tHe CrEATure[94] as it forced Kevin to the floor.

A thick band with a translucent backing.

Kevin, covered entirely, tried to push through its back.

It contracting rapidly, seemingly writhing around its trapped prey.

The back turned red.

Kevin's screaming stopped.[95]

"Move! Now!" Alex yelled.

Without hesitation, Alex, Alice, Josh, and Stuart turned and pushed out through the door, with Alex leading them towards the living quarters.

⁹⁶ This one says CHEATER.

⁹⁷ <This is not literal, obviously. This is likely more that the subject believes they know the answer somewhere deep down.>

⁹⁸ But something is blocking you from accepting the reasons.

⁹⁹ That, we think, will only happen if you come out of this with an acceptance of the guilt.

¹⁰⁰ This is actually a positive, apparently. It means that you're not looking outside yourself now, but rather only at the facets of yourself still in the Sim. You are trying to assign blame—or reason—internally. Keep fighting, Josh. I want us to be able to move forward, and we need a map for that. And I need to know that I was right to do what I did on some level. If this results in us being able to work things out, I can hold on to that.

SARAH WALKER: [Silent]

MARK TYLER: I understand this must be a shock.

SARAH WALKER: I…I don't know what to say. What was that thing?

MARK TYLER: We don't know for sure.

SARAH WALKER: You said that Ailuros may have intentionally withheld information. Did they know about it? THE…CReAturE?[96]

MARK TYLER: [Sighs] It's possible that at least one person did. They certainly should have been aware that the biological incident was not viral in nature.

SARAH WALKER: How so?

MARK TYLER: The final transmission from the unit commander was not very specific, but when taken in conjunction with the staff recordings from the moments just before and after the ejection, there was clearly something else going on. There is evidence that a full report[97] of what my husband found on board was sent to Thornton-Hythe, too, including files copied from the unit's internal systems. Our attempts to extract these—both wirelessly from the unit and physically from the company—have come up with a blank.[98]

SARAH WALKER: Can I hear any of the recordings you did retrieve?

MARK TYLER: As part of this particular session? No. If I can get clearance to include any of them in the case file though, you'll get to hear it when I send you your copy.[99]

SARAH WALKER: Okay. Thank you. Did we…did we see what happened to either Rob or Kevin? At the end?

MARK TYLER: No. Like Alice said, not all the cameras were functional. Once the terminal was damaged, the unit instigated an emergency protocol and started power cycling, keeping the monitoring systems active only where life was detected.[100] Or the monitoring systems that weren't already down anyway.

SARAH WALKER: Which means that Kevin was already dead when the others left the room.

MARK TYLER: I am afraid so, yes.

SARAH WALKER: [Pauses] I want to say something like 'at least it was quick,' but…it wasn't, was it? The way they screamed. And Kevin, you could see him struggling…My God.

MARK TYLER: Do you feel like you can continue, or would you like to take a break?

SARAH WALKER: What good would that do? I'd just have to face it again. No. Let's just keep going.

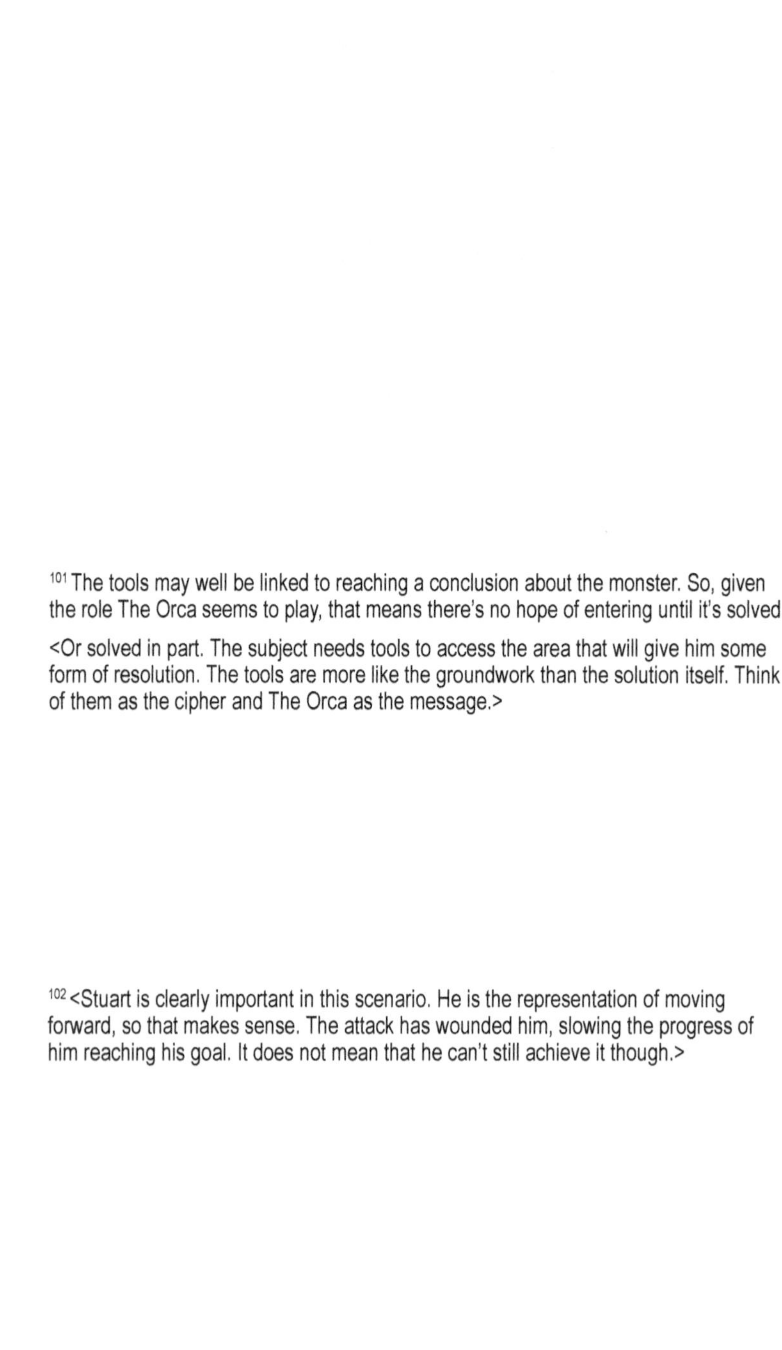

[101] The tools may well be linked to reaching a conclusion about the monster. So, given the role The Orca seems to play, that means there's no hope of entering until it's solved.

<Or solved in part. The subject needs tools to access the area that will give him some form of resolution. The tools are more like the groundwork than the solution itself. Think of them as the cipher and The Orca as the message.>

[102] <Stuart is clearly important in this scenario. He is the representation of moving forward, so that makes sense. The attack has wounded him, slowing the progress of him reaching his goal. It does not mean that he can't still achieve it though.>

Alex led Alice, Josh, and Stuart to a room that they'd searched with Kevin. The door was jammed half open which made it difficult to get inside. They hoped that it would be just as difficult for THE CREAture as it was for them. Just in case, once they were all inside, Alex pushed the door closed a little further, leaving a gap only big enough to look through.

"What was that thing?"

Alex gripped the door frame and tensed. They closed their eyes and concentrated on staying calm, though when they spoke, their voice cracked under the strain. "I suspect it may be the *biological incident.* Whatever it is though, it broke the control panel. There's no way we're getting the doors to The Orca open now. Not without tools, anyway."[101]

"Is there any way we can call for help?" Alice asked, turning to Stuart. "What about the emergency broadcast?"

"We have the code, so maybe. We'd need to get to the control room though. That should be—" Stuart tried to lift his arm to check the map, but a sharp inhale cut his words short.

Alex turned to look at the rookie and realized that he'd been gripping his arm all the time they'd been moving towards their current hiding spot. They floated over and pulled Stuart's fingers away a little, revealing a hand-length tear in his Skin Suit. Blood immediately started to rise from between the material.

Alex pressed Stuart's fingers back in place and stated, "We need to get you fixed up first.[102] Is the medical bay on this floor the only one?"

Stuart shook his head. "No. Someone call up a map."

Alice tapped her Wrist Display and called up the projection, holding it out to Stuart. Stuart looked it over and continued, "The units were all supposed to be identical. Ground level is living quarters and retail with some essential staff areas. Second level is the resort; dance hall, food hall, and key staffed areas. So…yes, there. Second floor medical. It should be larger than the ground floor one."

"The one on this floor is closer," Alice said.

Alex bit their lip. "That thing is also down here though."

Alice tapped a button and let the life sign scanner kick in on the map.

[103] We're working on the theory that the scanners not really synching up means that each fact would apply a different thinking to the monster and that none of them yet have a clear understanding. It actually makes death a good thing in the Sim. A facet dying means they are no longer needed to find an answer, at least in your mind. It's like a process of elimination thing.

"Yeah, but the life sign scanner is showing a lot of blips up on the second floor."

Alex called up the map on their own Wrist Display to get a better look. When the blips dropped into place though, something became apparent very quickly. "They still haven't synched up properly."[103]

Alice looked over the two maps, noting the differences in blip positions and shook her head. "With the terminal out of commission, I don't know if they will either."

"Shit," Alex replied. They let out a groan and ran a hand over their mouth, rubbing their cheeks while they thought things through. "Both *are* showing a lot more activity…Okay. Okay, we assume the worst and head to the one down here first. Puss-Puss, you okay?"

Josh nodded.

Alex pulled themselves down in front of Josh, forcing him to make eye contact, and asked, "Do you think you'll be able to stitch Stuart up when we get to medical?"

It took a moment for the words to sink in, but when they did, Josh blinked and looked over at Stuart's injury. "Yeah. Yeah, I should be. If they have supplies."

Alex nodded, and gave Josh a smile. "Okay. Good. Wait…the blips were on the second level."

"Well, duh," Alice replied, rolling her eyes. "Hence our heading for the med bay on this floor. What about it?"

"No, I mean, we definitely didn't misread them, right?" Alex checked their map again, groaned, and switched to comms. "Aaron. Lucy. Are you okay?"

After a moment of silence, Lucy responded, "Of course we're okay. Why wouldn't we be?"

"The biological incident wasn't a virus. We were attacked by... something."

Aaron laughed. "Of course you were. You idiots keep playing make believe, we'll get the real work done, yeah?"

Alice grabbed Alex's wrist and hissed, "We're not messing around. This *thing*…It killed Stockley. And…Rob…"

"Sure it did," Aaron said, drawing the words out in a mocking tone. "And your acting is award worthy."

Alice's cheeks flared with anger, and she growled, "Just check your fucking display. You should have access to the life sign scanner now. It's glitching but…The floor you're on might be crawling with these things."

There were another few seconds of silence, and Lucy came back on with,

"I just checked the hallway to, you know, catch a blip monster or whatever. Gotta love those false positives."

Stuart let out a quiet grunt, having now been able to lift his arm enough to check his own map. "The one that attacked us. It looks like it's heading up to the second level."

Alex balled their hand into a fist and pulled every bit of firmness they could into their voice. "Look...the thing that attacked us is heading your way. It broke the door controls, so we can't get back into The Orca. We're heading to the medical bay in the Northwest corner of the ground floor. Just meet us there, okay?"

Alex cut comms and turned back to the others. "Come on, let's get moving before that thing comes back."

[104] That makes sense. If I'm understanding this right, the Ego works more on logic than the Id, which is impulse driven.

[105] Clear Ego again, finding pleasure and a way to avoid negative consequences while still satisfying the urges of the Id.

Lucy followed Aaron into a side room and watched as he started grabbing at free floating packages. He checked one over, pushed it her way, and tore another one open, revealing a granola bar. The sign outside had said 'Pantry,' so of course they'd find food.

"I can't believe those idiots thought we'd fall for that," he said, chomping down on half the bar. "We were attacked. By something. Whooo. Scary. Fucking morons."

As far as Lucy was concerned, the problem with tools that can talk was that they often did talk, and far too much. And not think about things like whether a virus could be caught from food in a unit that had been abandoned due to a biological incident.[104] She shrugged and pushed the package away. "What do you expect? The Kembles never have taken this job seriously enough."

"Yeah. And Josh Byrne ain't been the same since he left Macey to die on that old war ship. Shacking up with the upper-class interloper hasn't helped him any, either."

Lucy noted that, for a post ejection unit, the pantry was still pretty well stocked. She thought about the numbers of people there and wondered what would kill that many people that quickly. Not that it mattered now.

Lucy pushed the thought away and asked, "What do you make of the newbies?"

"You should have seen Stockley back on The Orca," Aaron chuckled. "The little prick just hid in the corner when I was dealing with Rob and the rich kid. He's desperate to avoid confrontation, you can tell. He'd probably do anything to fit in with a group. I bet the other one's the same."

Lucy nodded at a heavy looking machine at the back of the room. "RX Ninety-three room temperature unit. The control boards go for a nice amount. Small too. Like tuck inside your skin suit small."[105]

Aaron smiled. "Then let's get it free and see if we can avoid it ending up on the salvage manifesto."

They both drifted over to the machine and started checking it over. Aaron gave the side a tap and said, "This looks like the main panel, here. We'll have to pry it open."

Aaron gripped the edges of the machine and tried to force it. When that

[106] <Again, in dreams, money often means self-confidence and self-worth. Seeing a photo of a happy family doesn't improve the subject's own happiness, so his Ego discards it. This might be a sign that his sole overriding goal right now is to reach a level of improvement in how he views himself. It may also explain why Lucy acts in a mercenary way.>

failed, he switched on his Mag Boots for extra leverage, but again, it wouldn't budge. Annoyance rising to his face, he switched tact and tried a series of kicks, causing a loud *bang, bang* to echo around the room.

Foster watched Aaron taking his aggression out on the machine and decided not to get involved. Instead, she moved to the side and started looking on top of the food storage lockers.

Reaching up, her fingers brushed metal and she pulled out a small tin. It opened with ease, but all it contained was a handful of photos of a man in a chef's hat, holding two smiling children. They had no monetary value, so she pushed them away.[106]

Lucy gripped the top of the lockers and made use of the microgravity environment, pulling herself up to get a better look. At the back, she could make out a shape in the shadows. She reached in and pulled out a small handgun. Lowering herself back down, she turned it over in her hand. *It's still loaded.*

Click-click-click.

The sound floated in, audible only between Aaron's continued kicking. Lucy stopped what she was doing and turned her head. Her eyes went wide. *Something* floated right by her, either unaware of her presence or focused solely on the noise that Aaron was making. The clicking, she realized, came from the quills that lined the inside of the ring which formed tHe CrEATure's body.

"Fucker's jammed on there tight," Aaron said, finally stopping his assault and turning back to Lucy. "If we find a crowbar or something, that would help. Is there anyth—What the fuck?"

Aaron forced himself hard back against the machine, but The CREATurE darted forward, trying to wrap itself around him. Somehow, he managed to wriggle an arm free and slammed his gloved hand into the thing's back. A bright flash illuminated the dully light room as Aaron activated his Shock Glove, and his attacker rippled free from his grip.

Its back now burned, tHE CreATure clattered its quills together in a cacophonous click-roar that echoed around the room.

Creeeeeee!

It whipped forward and forced Aaron to the floor, his screams rising above the sound of rapidly tearing flesh.

Lucy had seen enough. She raised the gun and took aim at the *thing*. She wrapped her finger around the trigger.

And, she paused.

[107] In part, this applies to the concept of the Ego as a logical thinker. My friend said it may go deeper than it seems, though. She had a chance to try to kill the monster. But she didn't. It may be that she understands the importance of it as a symbol and that not killing it is crucial to your self-preservation. As mercenary as the character of Lucy is, she is still a part of you that wants to find a suitable outcome. She may be framed as a villain here, but her overall goal is positive. As to Aaron's death, the monster is more focussed on one issue than Aaron was, but it still stems from a primal urge. Therefore, it disposed of the chaotic Id and took his place in the narrative. See? Process of elimination and consolidation of facts.

She lowered the weapon and tucked it into a pocket on her Skin Suit.

Slowly, silently, she slipped back out the door and left her salvage partner to his fate.

Even as his cries died out, Lucy felt no sorrow and no guilt. Instead, she was simply thoughtful.[107]

MARK TYLER: Do you mind if I jump back to something quickly?

SARAH WALKER: Go ahead.

MARK TYLER: It occurred to me that Alice didn't originally believe that her brother was dead. Why would that be?

SARAH WALKER: Does anybody ever want to believe that someone they care for is dead?

MARK TYLER: I was thinking more about the 'this again' comment.

SARAH WALKER: I wouldn't know the specifics. My guess? He's faked something similar on a job before. Rob is…was…a practical joker. He liked to make people smile, but nobody more than himself. As much as he didn't want to offend people, he could never quite draw the line between a joke and upset.

MARK TYLER: Did he ever prank you?

SARAH WALKER: Once. With itching powder, of all things.

MARK TYLER: That doesn't sound too bad.

SARAH WALKER: He put it on the toilet paper in Alice's bathroom just before I went in.

MARK TYLER: Ah.

SARAH WALKER: Honestly, I thought he was mad at me for not wanting date number two at first. It turned out he just thought it was funny. And if it made someone laugh, even if just himself, then why would anyone be upset? So, no I don't know what he did to warrant that response, but he was certainly capable of faking his own death.

MARK TYLER: Moving on, with their background in pharmaceuticals, I would have thought that Alex was a better choice to patch Stuart up. Was he offering it to Josh to give him something to focus on, do you think?

[108] Okay, so this has a lot to do with the roles of the characters. Stuart, your hope to move forward, needs patching up. In the story, you are more qualified to do that. In reality, that's also the case. You're not trying to fix any larger issues with us, you're trying to fix your own issues. You have to be the one to do that. That it's me that prompts you here is probably because you know the issues affect me too. It's also possible that part of you is sort of aware what is happening. Having a forced Neg-Vac would mean that some things that are normally present—such as paranoia (which would be justified in this instance, I suppose)—were supressed and are now bubbling up.

[109] Case in point, you're right. I don't know how to fix you.

[110] This is another obvious one. Like I said, Macey represented your relationship with him. After you split, you were hurting, and you started, well, wallowing from what I heard. And going for people that you could control. I guess the lack of control you felt with him made you crave something you could keep in check? Not that you were good at that. You were already going a little off the rails with the alcohol then, too. When we started dating, you really did chill out a bit. Until our friends did what they did.

[111] Again, our friends weren't great. Yours at least disappeared pretty quickly, I suppose. Mine didn't really know when to stop.

[112] Is that how relationships feel to you right now? If it is, that hurts too. I tried, Josh. I really did.

SARAH WALKER: That was probably part of it. Josh is better qualified, too.[108] Alex knows what they're looking at, what drugs to load up—or sell—but they don't know how to use the equipment.[109] You saw how Josh operated the tattoo table, right? They aren't as straight forward as he made it look. He can do the same with automated med stations. And if the medical table doesn't work, he can do things by hand, at least to a point.

MARK TYLER: Interesting. Did he start out in the medical field?

SARAH WALKER: [Frowns] With how much doctors earn these days, do you really think he'd step away from that for this? No. He and Macey used to take on what would be termed 'risky jobs.' When you do that, you have to pick up how to patch each other up, or you fall apart.

MARK TYLER: Does he still take risky jobs?

SARAH WALKER: He did. After Macey's death, he started taking the toughest ones he could for a little while. Then Alex came along, and he calmed down a bit.[110]

MARK TYLER: The concept that he was somehow to blame for Macey's death has come up a few times now. Even with it not being the case, so many people saying it was his fault must have left him questioning whether it was.

SARAH WALKER: He felt guilty before the talk started. When people started pinning the blame on him, too? I was worried that he was trying to get himself killed. It was a situation that wasn't nice for anyone. Josh blamed himself already, and the majority of the people who pushed that angle didn't believe it and were lashing out. Over time, it just stuck.

MARK TYLER: Actions speak louder than words, but words echo longer in the dark.[111]

SARAH WALKER: And it doesn't get much darker than the big, black beyond.[112]

MARK TYLER: This will sound a little strange, I'm sure, but I'm pretty sure he wasn't trying to get himself killed.

SARAH WALKER: Now I'm curious. What makes you say that?

[113] That's interesting. It's an open acknowledgement of what you did. Thinking about it, maybe that's why you sucked at being controlling? You set yourself up to be in destructive relationships but never took that final step?

[114] Okay, I'm going to step up a little here, too. When I saw the two of you together, it was only a few hours before my next Neg-Vac. I intentionally skipped it. I felt like I was processing what I saw and I knew that taking the injection would push it all back again. It's funny really. Neither of us fully believed the thinking behind them. Most crime is attributable to particular negative emotions. Greed, jealousy, low self-esteem. Some things, like anger and assault are obvious correlations, right? But a lot of it seems kinda flimsy. Yet, I skip one Neg-Vac and what do I do? All of this. Maybe it's an almost trained response due to all the propaganda. Or maybe I'm the proof of the system being correct. But hey. This is me being honest. Just like your unconscious did via Mark.

[115] My friend said this definitely means you knew that the Comic Con was a ticketed event, and you knew there was a risk of getting caught.

MARK TYLER: The last time I felt guilty over something *big*, I took a similar course of action. For me, I drank. Heavily. Then, I put myself in position where I *could* fall. The roofs of buildings, tall bridges, that sort of thing. The thing was, I never took that final step to the edge. I had kinda convinced myself that I had left it to fate, but really, I was keeping myself in check. When you think about it, the nature of salvaging means that Josh would have had plenty of opportunities to die. If he had really wanted to, he would have.[113]

SARAH WALKER: Honestly, I thought the same. We all have limits though. If he'd been pushed enough, he may have stepped over the edge.

MARK TYLER: [Nods] Alex appears to be taking charge quite effectively here.

SARAH WALKER: I noticed that. I'm glad. Stuart was hurt, Alice lost her brother, and Josh was in shock. Alex stepped up.[114]

MARK TYLER: Does that surprise you?

SARAH WALKER: Not really. Alex comes across as naturally submissive, but they've always had a thick skin. The strength was there, they just didn't like conflict. You should see them when it comes to physical performance art. They really know how to lead a crowd.

MARK TYLER: Oh?

SARAH WALKER: Dancefloors and microgravity obstacle courses. It's hard not to get drawn in watching them there. I don't think Alex even knows they're doing it, but they have people glued to them.

MARK TYLER: Huh. Well that makes sense. [Coughs] Okay, moving on, what did you think of what happened with Colt and Foster?

SARAH WALKER: [Sighs] I guess I got my evidence of rule-breaking. Why the idiots would do it in front of a camera is beyond me.

MARK TYLER: They'd already left when Alice mentioned synching the cameras up to The Orca. Nobody told them, and there was nothing that would give it away.[115]

[116] <The Guild itself houses all the facets. It seems likely that it represents the subject's own moral framework. Therefore, cheating would be breaking the Guild rules. That he said 'if' they'd succeeded points towards him perhaps not 'going all the way.' The whole Sim is a little contradictory in that way, though. It's likely that he did something, but didn't go as far as he could have.>

You know it was wrong, but you aren't sure how big a crime it was. For me, it's a big one, Josh. Still, I suppose I should take this as a small mercy. You know that it's still cheating, but you aren't sure how far against your own views on a relationship it goes.

[117] I'm glad you acknowledge that on some level. You could have left long before you did. That you didn't shows the sort of person you are. In more ways than one.

SARAH WALKER: Of course. Yeah, they were already gone when the cameras linked up, weren't they? Damn.

MARK TYLER: Is what they were doing a major issue in terms of the Guild rules?

SARAH WALKER: If they'd succeeded, then yes.[116] It would have been outright theft. I wouldn't say they were lucky, though, given the only reason they failed was…well.

MARK TYLER: And Foster did nothing.

SARAH WALKER: [Pauses] What could she have done? Okay, she had a gun. But that opens up three issues. One, the reasons for the no firearms ruling. Two, she doesn't know if it would be effective. That the gun is there might indicate that it was never tried, but it could also indicate that this thing is bullet proof. And three, she knows it's loaded, or she wouldn't have pointed it, but she doesn't know that it would definitely fire after being left alone there for however long it was.

MARK TYLER: So, do you think she made the right decision?

SARAH WALKER: Most times, you make sure you both get out alive. Then there's that one in a thousandth moment where you can't. If she believed that there was even a chance that this was that moment, then making sure one of them got out to tell the tale was more important.

MARK TYLER: Was that the same with Josh and Macey?

SARAH WALKER: It was. The difference is, Josh tried to save her. But he wouldn't have been wrong not to.[117]

MARK TYLER: Let's keep going.

[118] <Mental barriers to protect the subject, and the need to be able to dig into them when ready.>

[119] You've spent a long time building walls to keep the really bad stuff out. Is that because of the Neg-Vac system, I wonder? I know it just suppresses stuff, but what I mean is, did you intentionally avoid dealing with things because part of you thinks the system would have helped, but without it, you can't deal with it all properly?

The crew made their way up the main hallway as fast as they could. When they reached the medical bay, the door lights were already powered on. Josh hit the release button and the door slid to the side, but behind it sat a pile of crates. He gave one a tentative push. It wouldn't budge.

"A blockade is standard protocol in case of an emergency," Stuart said. "You need to be able to move it though, so the magnetization buttons should be on whichever side you can reach."[118]

Josh and Alice started working their arms around the barricade, searching for the release on the largest crate. The moment they touched it, the box began to float up a little, and they were able to push it aside and scramble inside.

Josh guided Stuart across the room and Alex and Alice took up position by the door. Alice glanced out into the hallway and said, "If this stuff wasn't disturbed, that thing probably couldn't get in. Help me get it all back in place."

Alex nodded and pushed the large box back into place, re-engaging the lock once it was fully blocking the gap again. It pulled to the floor with a loud *thunk*.

Alice grimaced at the sound and frantically returned her gaze to the open doorway. Alex joined her and, once they were both sure that the hallway was still empty, they shut the door from the inside. The box was a little further forward in one corner now though, and the door stopped short of fully shutting. "It's probably better that we can see the hallway anyway," she said. "There's no way that thing is getting through that gap anyway."[119]

Meanwhile, Josh helped Stuart into the only examination chair in the room and peeled down the top of his Skin Suit. He wrapped a strap around Stuart to keep him—and most importantly, his arm—in place. Looking over the wound, Josh could see that Stuart was cut in several places. The wounds looked pretty deep, too.

Josh nodded at a large robotic arm that peered around the side of the chair. "Okay. That's an automated med arm over there. Do you know how they work?"

Stuart shook his head and gripped his wound with his free hand. "Not really, no."

"It would scan your body for injuries, then perform the relevant procedure.

[120] That ties into what I just noted, doesn't it? You're worried about how far to push things when it comes to dealing them. And fears about whether the Neg-Vac system would or wouldn't help.

[121] <The subject's body may have picked up on the Neg-Vac injection and that it wasn't custom built for them.>

[122] You need my help to deal with this. That much is true. Depending how this all plays out, I suppose I'll be the final turning point for you? What I decide to do will dictate whether you face this alone or with me. I knew that already, I guess. Having it pointed out feels odd though. Scary too. It's easier if I place the focus on myself in that regard and don't think about what it would do to you if I left.

[123] My friend put this down to you viewing my dancing around the issue as not trying to hurt you too much. That works if they're right that part of you knew that I probably knew. Part of me did want to hurt you, I think. Because you hurt me. So, I'm sorry, but I'm not that nice, not in this instance.

That's if it's got everything loaded in the arm. I can do that if you like, but…the problem is, it'll potentially read this damage and put you under. If it does that, I don't know how long you'll be out for, especially if it doesn't have anything loaded to wake you.[120] It'd be noisy too. Quick, but noisy."

Stuart winced and gripped his arm tighter. "Do I have any other options?"

"I can do it by hand."

"Have you done it before?"

"A couple of times. It'll be hard to judge anesthetic levels though."[121]

Stuart took a deep breath and exhaled. He was certain of his choice. Scared, but certain. "You do it. I don't want to risk being out if that thing comes back."

Josh nodded. "Alex, can you check for anesthetic?"[122]

"Sure," they replied.

Josh started searching the nearby drawers. He was glad to find that they were laid out in a logical order, making it easier to find the needle and thread.

At the same time, Alex checked the vials of liquid displayed at the back of the room. Once they'd found a suitable dosage, they loaded it into a small injection gun and handed it to Josh. They leaned in and whispered, "This should do it. It's probably a little too small a dose, but I didn't want to risk knocking him out entirely."[123]

Josh gave them a little smile and returned to the examination chair. He pulled a pipe out from underneath it and showed it to Stuart. "This is to keep the blood from floating out in the room. It's kinda like the little vacuum things dentists use. The anesthetic will only work in the area it's injected, so once you feel it start to go numb, I'll need you to take this with your other hand and move it around the wound, okay?"

"Okay," Stuart replied.

Josh let the pipe go, leaving it to float freely next to them. He pressed a few buttons on the injection gun, reading the small display as he cycled through options. Once satisfied, he pressed it against Stuart's injured arm and pulled the trigger.

Stuart grit his teeth, but his arm soon stopped tensing, and he began to relax a little. He took the pipe and started focussing on keeping the blood from spreading in the air.

"That's hopefully going to numb it, but even then you're still going to feel this," Josh confirmed. "It's going to be disorientating if you watch, like you know it's happening but not really. Try not to pay attention to what I'm doing. Just keep the suction pipe moving in a circle around the area."

[124] Your whole relationship with him was to a point, wasn't it? Excitement is addictive. And he offered that.

[125] This relates to your actions after the split, I think.

[126] How long into the relationship with him was it before you questioned how you got to where you were?

Stuart swallowed hard and turned his head away, eyes darting around the room.

Josh raised the needle and pressed it against Stuart's arm, pushing it through his skin.

Alex noticed Stuart clench his jaw and said, "There's a lot of stuff in here. I'm going to have a look through it. If the door was blocked, maybe there'll be something useful in the file storage. Stuart, why don't you tell us a little about what you did on Ailuros? It might help keep your mind focused."

Stuart closed his eyes. "I was…one of the guests, at first. I'd finished up with college and didn't have any real goals in life, so I took a holiday. Have you ever stayed on Ailuros?"

"No," Josh replied, focusing on pulling his wounds closed.

"It's intoxicating.[124] If you're staying there for fun, it's a non-stop party. The company that runs it, uhm, Thornton-Hythe, I think? They even allow some monitored, mild drug use if you want hallucinogens. You know, to make it really exciting."

Without moving from her place by the door, Alice asked, "So why the switch to working there? Did you enjoy it that much?"

"Not really. I was there because I had no direction in life, and it didn't do anything to help that.[125] Eventually, my pre-paid time ran out. So, I topped it up. More than once. The money ran out in the end, and I couldn't even get home. My dad was pissed. Mum wanted him to pay for me to come back, but he wouldn't do it. He said it was my problem to sort."

"Sounds harsh," Josh said.

"It was needed, in a way. What he did was force me to examine how I'd gotten to where I was.[126] I did a couple of odd jobs for the resort to pay for my room and came up with a compromise. Dad agreed to fund a training course for me. That way, I could earn my way back."

"What course was it?"

"Food Production Technician."

Alice chuckled. "Isn't that just a fancy term for a vending machine repair man? Was that your choice?"

"No. It was dad's. I thought it was pretty bad, too, until I started working on it. Right up to that first class, I was thinking 'this is just until I get enough cash to get home. It's a sucky job, but at least I'm getting paid.' That's what I told myself. Then I saw how in depth it was."

Josh raised a curious eyebrow. "In depth? Really?"

"It's not all cleaning nozzles in the 3D food printers. You need to

[127] This is all personal. You needed to fix the hardware/physical stuff (coming off the alcohol) and the software/internal stuff (emotional thought processes) before you could start to move on. Then, you found me.

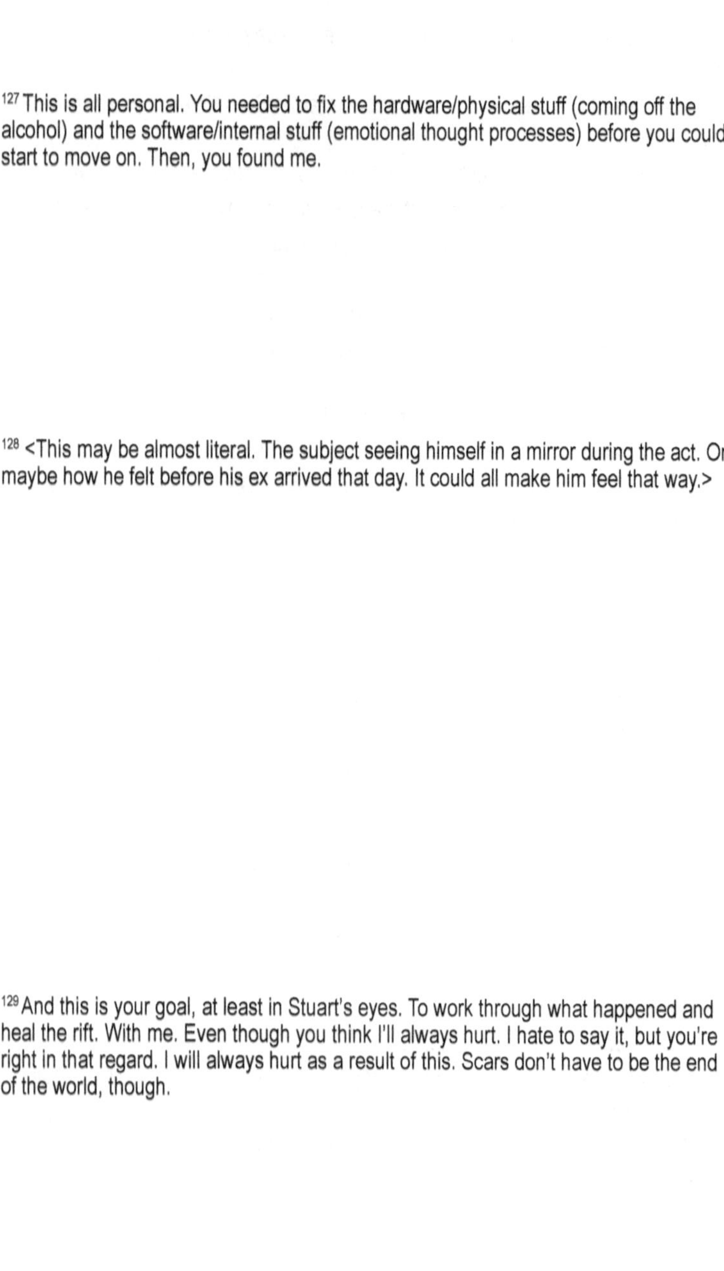

[128] <This may be almost literal. The subject seeing himself in a mirror during the act. Or maybe how he felt before his ex arrived that day. It could all make him feel that way.>

[129] And this is your goal, at least in Stuart's eyes. To work through what happened and heal the rift. With me. Even though you think I'll always hurt. I hate to say it, but you're right in that regard. I will always hurt as a result of this. Scars don't have to be the end of the world, though.

understand how to identify and fix problems with both the hardware and the software. There's a lot more programming involved than I expected. Electrician work too. The course actually took longer than the security courses there."[127]

"So what you're saying," Alice replied, "Is you could have been more help than you were back at the terminal?"

"You seemed to be enjoying it."

She rolled her eyes. "Did you pass?"

"I did. I could have stayed on afterwards, too, but by then, I was sick of the sight of the place. When you stop partying, but you're around all the people that are…"

Josh nodded. "It's like watching a video of yourself drunk. Or catching sight of yourself in the mirror when you have just enough sense left to understand what you're doing, but not enough to stop it."[128]

"Something like that. I figured that the course at least left me some transferable skills though, so I hopped a ship back to Earth. The problem was, I couldn't use the qualification. The microgravity focus meant that part of it was next to useless on Earth, and Thorton-Hythe had the course custom built to be unique to Ailuros and their other resorts. It was legal, because it was legitimate, but it wasn't recognized anywhere else."

"And you couldn't stand the idea of going back again," Josh added.

"No. Salvaging was pretty much the only career that would take me without having to start over from scratch with the training."

Josh tied the thread and gave Stuart's shoulder a reassuring squeeze. "And we're done. What does your dad think of you doing this stuff?"

"Thank you," Stuart said, releasing the pipe and starting to loosen the straps. "And I haven't told him. I was kinda hoping this salvage would make me more than just my living expenses and I'd be able to show that to him and say look what I achieved. I doubt he'll ever be proud of me after Ailuros, but you never know."[129]

"Well, look who it is," Alice said, peering through the small gap left by the door. She disabled the electromagnet on largest crate again and moved it out of the way, then opened the door. She watched Lucy float in in silence, then checked the hallway and shut the door again. "Where's Colt?"

Lucy shook her head, still eerily quiet, and moved to the corner of the room.

"Until we have a solid plan, we may as well hole up," Alice mumbled, and locked the crate back in place, this time with the door shut entirely.

A heavy dread hung over the team. They were all aware that they needed

¹³⁰ Did you know? Were you aware what I was doing? The 'sample' is possibly representative of me seeing part of what happened. No, apparently not. The listening to audio is more likely you wanting to read this report to see if that helps make sense of things. The keeping the volume low is a way to hide. My friend says that means you were considering keeping it from me. The sample is another nod towards you not doing everything you'd maybe intended—or expected—when he arrived. You sampled the things on offer, but didn't take a full plate.

to figure out what they were up against. To that end, Josh turned to the filing room at the far end of the bay and asked, "Hey, Alex. Find anything useful?"

After a moment, Alex pulled themselves back into the room, their face pale, and holding a box the length of their forearm in one hand. They opened it and pulled out what appeared to be a thick strip of flesh with a layer of spines hanging out of one side.

"What the hell is that?" Josh asked.

Lucy looked over at the strip and held out her hand. Alex handed it over, and she started carefully running her fingers over the spines, apparently testing their sharpness.

Alex wrinkled their face and said, "I think it's a…sample. I found a USB stick that has the same reference number. It's labelled as an audio summary. If we keep the volume low, the video might be useful."[130]

Everybody—apart from Lucy—looked at each other. It was Alice that broke the silence, stating plainly, "The door *is* blocked."

"It's a risk," Josh said, then shook his head. "No, anything we can learn is useful. Does anyone have any objections to us playing this thing?"Nobody said another word.

Josh nodded to Alex, and they slotted the stick into the side of their Wrist Display. They switched to holographic projection and hit play.

My name is Dr. Michalas. I am the last remaining medical examiner on Ailuros Unit Twenty-Three. Well. I am the last remaining person on board now. I've locked myself inside the ground floor medical bay. My days consist of supply runs and, sometimes, sleep. Those things can't get through my barricade. When I leave to pick up food, I have to get it back in place from the outside so that none of them get in while I'm away.

I'm tired. Too tired. I'll make a mistake and I won't make it back. I can feel it coming. It should ensure they don't accidentally damage this stick though. It's the only one holding this file. There's no point sending it to all of them. Not now, anyway.

I tried to contact the Ailuros main hub. They accepted the call, but I couldn't get an auditory response. I thought initially that there was a system error, so I simply ran through what I knew. Then, less than twenty-four hours later, systems started shutting down. Not all of them, but certainly a lot of them. In a regimented order. Computers, one by one, started wiping files. In order.

For a while the cameras appeared to be transmitting to the Control Room, but where the footage was stored, I don't know. When I saw what was happening, I amplified our general location beacon, but I don't know if it's still transmitting. Eventually, all communications were locked out. From what I can tell, the main life support systems are still in place, and I can work with the power consumption and other basic functions. Nothing that you wouldn't find in a house though. And some things you would aren't working anymore.

It *had* to be the central hub. They must have done something. I just don't know why. If I were to guess, I'd say that I've been abandoned. The company saw what they were dealing with and decided that it would be better to ride it out. Frankly, my hope is that when somebody finds this unit, tHE...CREATures will have already died out. This report is simply...

I don't really have anything to leave anyone. Not on here, anyway. This summary of my findings is the best I can do. Please understand though; I'm a trainee in human medical practises, not an expert in animal biology. As such, much of this is untested guesswork born of observations and comparisons to what little files we hold on Earth wildlife.

THE CreAtures did not come from Ailuros. That should be obvious. We're more akin to a pleasure cruise than a biological research base. No. We were due a supply drop, but when the ship arrived, it docked on autopilot. That isn't necessarily unusual, but nobody was answering on comms. Commander Sheffield took a small security team to the hanger to investigate.

There were three of those things on board, and within the first ten minutes of them entering the unit, they had killed six people. The Commander escaped and, understandably, panicked. Rather than request assistance, he declared the unit a biohazard and ejected us into open space.

We tried at first to contain the threat, gathering people into safe rooms and leaving the security teams to hunt the things down. As you have no doubt guessed, we failed to eradicate the threat. Even when the various incarnations of the security team managed to catch one with a suppression net, it proved to be deadly to deal with unless we turned up the charge on it. When they did finally kill one though, I was the only medical practitioner left. As such, I had the honour of examining the corpse.

THE fully grown CreAtuREs all seem to be of a similar size. The specimen we caught had the following measurements when stretched into a near circle. Body radius, three feet. Body diameter, six feet. Body circumference, eighteen point eight-five feet. Body area, twenty-eight point two-seven square feet. The main band was approximately half an inch thick, with the attached backing around one quarter of an inch in thickness.

When cut open, the ring that forms tHE CreATures' primary body can be peeled like an onion. It appears to have six layers. As best as I can tell, they are as follows. The outer most skin is roughly one point five millimetres thick. It feels leathery to touch but is deceptively stretchy. Beneath this is a layer of muscle tissue, measuring two point two millimetres in thickness. Next appears to be the brain. This is two point five millimetres in thickness and runs the entire length of the ring.

Next is a two point three-millimetre-thick layer that houses what I am assuming are the internal organs. They sit within a gelatinous substance broadly similar to our own areolar connective tissue. As with the brain, these are stretched to match the body shape. Based on my research of animals that practice hematophagy, digestion appears to be broadly similar in nature to that of a vampire bat.

Finally, we have another two point five millimetre layer of muscle tissue and a one point seven-millimetre-thick layer of skin, both of which are identical in nature to the outer two layers.

The quill-like protrusions that line the inner ring run to around four point five inches in length and sit in lines of eight. While not barbed, they are not dissimilar to porcupine quills. They certainly share the hardened layer of keratin if nothing else. Observations show them as likely having several uses. The primary one is to pierce the skin of prey and draw blood when feeding or defending itself.

It is worth noting that there are small holes around the base of the quills. This is where waste excretions take place, pushing a paste-like substance up and out their length. The substance is quite thick, but slippery. Whether intended or not, it certainly acts as a lubricant for the quills, making piercing easier.

THe CreAturEs also rub and clatter the quills together to create a variety of sounds. The primary noise, a cacophonous click-roar, was initially thought to be a form of intimidation, targeted at prey. While this remains likely, I believe there may be more to it than this.

Again, this is all theory based on what little observations I have been able to make, but...the inner side of the ring is covered with small, fine hairs. Without a dead specimen to study, I would never have noticed them. They are soft to touch and hold some similarities to those found on arachnids and insects. My theory is that they work as trichobothria, allowing tHe CreATurEs to read both the sounds around them and movements from a substantial distance.

This makes sense given their lack of visible eyes or ears. From watching the footage of tHe cREATurEs caught on the working cameras, it appears that they are capable of creating a 'ping' noise by flicking two quills together. This may well be part of a pseudo echolocation. Maybe.

I've also noticed that they rarely rattle all the quills at once—unless attacking—and instead use small segments. Though the noise is the same as if they used any of the quills, it appears that it's the position of them in relation to their body that matters.

For example, if it were to rattle a three centimetre section of quills in the most northerly part of its ring, it would continue to do so while rotating, simply alternating which quills are moving to ensure that the sound comes from the same point positionally. In practise, it is often more complicated than this single point, however. THE CreAtures often click several points at once, sometimes in sequence.

It may be that this is a form of language for them. I like to think of it as… think of the ring as a page in a book. The top section is the start of the page, and the words, or clicks, travel across it coherently. Take the sample that

should be housed with this stick. When THE CReAurE died, the quills went rigid. These were the only ones that had moved. The pattern is as follows, from left to right, starting at the first row:

Straight, Up, Straight, Straight, Up, Straight, Straight, Straight.
Straight, Up, Up, Straight, Straight, Up, Straight, Up.
Straight, Up, Up, Straight, Up, Up, Straight, Straight.
Straight, Up, Up, Up, Straight, Straight, Straight, Straight.
Straight, Straight, Up, Straight, Straight, Straight, Straight, Straight.
Straight, Up, Straight, Up, Straight, Straight, Straight, Straight.
Straight, Up, Up, Straight, Straight, Straight, Straight, Up.
Straight, Up, Up, Straight, Up, Straight, Straight, Up.
Straight, Up, Up, Straight, Up, Up, Up, Straight.
Straight, Straight, Up, Straight, Straight, Straight, Straight, Straight.
Straight, Up, Straight, Straight, Up, Straight, Up, Up.
Straight, Up, Up, Straight, Up, Straight, Straight, Up.
Straight, Up, Up, Straight, Up, Up, Straight, Straight.
Straight, Up, Up, Straight, Up, Up, Straight, Straight.
Straight, Straight, Up, Straight, Straight, Straight, Straight, Straight.
Straight, Up, Straight, Straight, Up, Up, Straight, Up.
Straight, Up, Up, Straight, Straight, Up, Straight, Up.

Moving on, ThE CreATure's back is flexible, almost rubber like. While not as tough as the main band, it is still impossible to tear by hand. It appears to act as a spine equivalent, allowing tHE CREATures to keep some shape. The important parts are these sphincter-like protrusions.

These serve two purposes. The fleshy part around the holes is absorbent and is where tHE CreATuREs take in blood during a feed. This is aided by the suction effect of the hole itself. The same hole appears on both sides of the layer. When alive, the holes are actually in constant use, puckering quietly every few seconds. By filtering a small amount of liquid dye into the air, I was able to study the purpose of this firsthand.

The hole on the inside of the band takes in oxygen—they seem to breathe this the same as we do—and the back hole pushes a portion of it back through to create a propulsion effect. This accounts for their ease of movement in microgravity. I suspect that the proportion taken in also helps push the absorbed blood around, perhaps by way of an internal massage of sorts.

The reproductive cycles of THe CreAturEs are relatively simple. They each have four wombs that sit between the flesh layers of the band. I was

fortunate in that we caught the one we did before the young could become fully formed. ThE CrEAturEs are born pregnant. When they feed, blood enters here into a small sac, then undoubtedly filters in to the unborn.

The babies remain in the womb until their back layers are formed and their quills are fully hardened. The process is similar to adactylidium mites, but with a creation more closely aligned to aphids during an asexual reproductive cycle.

Even before the cameras stopped recording, we were unable to catch a birth on video. Not that you'd want to see it. These things live around four to six months, then the babies—all of which usually mature at a similar rate—eat their way out. Their mother becomes their first real meal.

After that, they reach full grown size within three weeks. When one dies, four more replace it. The ones that first arrived here were nearly ready to give birth too...we were over-run pretty quickly.

Dr. Michalas chuckles.

They thought I was mad with this, but...I watched every bit of footage I could. The babies follow the exact hunting patterns that their mother did. They literally move through the same rooms in the same order. They communicate with the same *others* that their mother did too, and sleep in the same places. They only start to show a divergence in habits when external stimuli causes them to do so.

I ran a test on the partially formed babies in the one we caught. Their DNA was almost identical to that of the mother. They're clones, I'm certain of it. These things live to feed, grow their young, and expire, leaving behind four other versions of themselves.

And that's not even the scariest part. These things are built for this exact environment. Animals, to my knowledge, don't evolve to function this well in microgravity. Think about that. If these things weren't born, but were built, then what else is out there, and why would they make something so...

He sighs.

That's about all I can tell you. So, I'll leave you with this. Yesterday, the last remaining other survivor died, killed by one of those monsters. He was a member of the security team and he died saving me. He took a keen interest in my research, and wanted me to be able to compile this, for whatever it's worth.

In a way, I think he held a fondness for THEse CReAtuREs. Anyway. He wrote a poem about them. So. In memory of Francis Solomon, I give you 'The Devourer of All.'

[131] This whole report was fascinating. My friend was going to make notes, but I'd rather it came from me here. If nothing else, it will test my understanding.

On a base level, the monster is a mix of things that scared you. Bits of spiders, blood, etc. The creature definitely represents what you did with him, which means you're scared. Scared that it happened? Scared it could happen again? Scared that you don't know why it happened? Scared about what it will mean for us? I don't know. Maybe all of it, maybe none of it.

The fast life cycle and the way the creatures create clones of themselves means that the cycle of thinking that caused this happens a lot for you. And it builds and grows. The way they communicate plays into the same thing. They're noisy. And the more of them there are, the noisier they are. Not only that, but that it's always the same part of them that is used means that it's always the same sort of thing that goes through your head. You might know this already, but the common theory is that dreaming about being eaten is a sign that you're consumed by your sex drive. The line that ends the poem, 'Demands to be fed,' means you feel like it constantly screams at you to embrace that desire.

Dr. Michalas, we figured was your last line of defence against it. He was the last bit of you fighting to stop the creature from taking over. And now he's dead. Which again, confirms that you failed to combat it, at least to a point.

I want to be angry about that. The way this all reads though, you're in a cycle of suffering. We all have times that feel like that, I think. Yours is extreme though. The worst thing is, I knew you were suffering a little. Just not how much. Now I'm questioning if I missed something obvious. And beating myself up for selfishly trying to project it all onto me when this is the most 'about you' part of the whole thing.

It ripples gently in the air,
Quills bristling like a million tiny fingers.
Grasping.
Reaching.
Touching the fine, sensitive hairs that gather the scents of the world around them.
The eyeless demon knows its land by no more than shifts in the air.
But take heed dear friends and do not wander near,
Lest you wish to see those needles close in around you,
To feel your flesh shredded,
As the damnable thing contracts and expands,
Writhing in its bounty.
Blood.
The membranous backing to its body craves blood,
The hungry, wet sucking of its holes drowning out the screams of its prey.
This is not a time to be foolhardy.
Leave now.
Leave and never return.
For this is a death that cannot see,
A death that cannot hear.
Yet it feels you.
Starving.
Craving.
Fool, it knows you are here still.
And the devourer of all,
Demands to be fed.[131]

[132] <This is actually a flight response.>

Like fight or flight. What Alice is suggesting is essentially to run away from the problem.

[133] Remember, money equals self-worth. Lucy is suggesting taking the creature—which means fully accepting it—and using it to grow. The "fuck the Guild" line probably exists because part of you has just suggested that you leave it be, meaning some part of your moral system thinks that would be fine. Lucy is the hero here. She is trying to guide you.

[134] <The subject's Ego is impatient. She wants this to be dealt with. And swiftly. Possibly because she can see the other facets wanting to run.>

The file ended and the silence hung in the air.

"Leave now. Leave and never return. That sounds like a good plan," Alice said, balling her hand into a fist. "We need to find some tools, get back on The Orca, disengage, and never come back."[132]

Alex copied the file to their Wrist Display and said, "Agreed."

A single, loud *cla-click* replied to the thought and everybody turned to see that Lucy had now drawn the handgun. She was pointing it right at them, waving it slowly from person to person.

Josh raised his hands, gently pushing them towards Lucy in a soothing motion. "Foster...where did you get that?"

Lucy pulled her lips back into a feral grin. "Are you fucking insane? Actual. Alien. Life. This is the ultimate salvage."

Alice shook her head. "Are you fucking insane? There's no way the Guild would—"

"Fuck the Guild," Lucy cut in. "If we capture one of these things and take it to black market, we'll be made for life."[133]

"If you fire that gun and miss, it's going to put a hole in the unit," Alex replied, their voice slow and measured. "I don't know if the system is operational enough to account for the air leak. It might just dump the oxygen in an attempt to counter it. Or it may go on full lockdown until the hole is repaired."

Lucy tilted her head, the smile still on her face. "If I pull the trigger, you won't want to get out of the way then, will you? Here's what's going to happen. We're going to boot up the life sign scanners, find out where that thing is, and catch it. Then we're going to get out of here."

She nodded to Stuart. "You. The recording mentioned a suppression net. Load the map and show me where the security office is."

Stuart pulled the map projection up on his Wrist Display and tapped a room. "There."

"Two rooms down. Good. Now, boot up the life sign scan." Stuart did as requested and Lucy pulled up her own scanner. She looked from one to the other. "Real time scans are close enough to a match. Good. Now, get that junk out of the way so we can get this done."[134]

[135] You're working through the idea that the cheating and how you're feeling about it aren't part of the healthy lifestyle we're told is normal. That's a good thing.

[136] Read as potentially desired by you.

[137] You don't want to accept that.

[138] Again, you knew I'd find out.

MARK TYLER: Let's start with the report. What did you make of Dr. Michalas' findings?

SARAH WALKER: I'm not qualified to comment on that.

MARK TYLER: Nor am I. I'd still like to know your thoughts, though. With something like this, it's hard not to consider things, isn't it?

SARAH WALKER: I mean, what he's saying makes sense. His thinking is all very Earth-centric though. He's drawn analogues to the animals he's familiar with. Even the idea that it moves through microgravity by pushing air out the back is similar to the old NASA packs they had astronauts wear on space walks. If this thing really is an alien lifeform, then there's no guarantee that it would be bound by the rules of our own wildlife and creations.[135]

MARK TYLER: I agree with your core point. Dr. Michalas even said himself that he is working on knowledge he was able to find and that it's mostly speculation. You said 'if' though. If not alien, what else would it be?

SARAH WALKER: I don't know.

MARK TYLER: Given the apparent similarities with Earth creatures, you could argue that it's a potential human creation.[136]

SARAH WALKER: [Shakes her head] No.[137] We don't have the technology to create something like that. That's not something you could keep secret.[138]

MARK TYLER: Good. I'm glad you said that. I think we can agree, too, that the plan to leave and never come back was the correct approach. Can you comment on Lucy Foster's actions here? I know you wanted to see the positives in her when it came to what happened to Aaron Colt, but this is different, isn't it?

[139] It did. She recognized that you were ready to run and saw that that would result in negative consequences emotionally and in relation to your general social position. Your Ego is moving you towards pleasure, i.e. resolving your issues.

[140] <The subject has likely felt like they were on track before, but fallen. Likely multiple times.>

This is a sad line.

[141] <Losing his way of thinking about the creature, at least. That is what this will come down to. At this point, the best scenario would be for Lucy and at least one creature to survive. Failing that, if Lucy dies but a creature survives, there is still hope for acceptance, but only if any other survivors find a way to deal with it without killing it.>

In other words, no creatures surviving means you ran from what happened. And only creatures surviving means you feel consumed by it and can't resolve it.

SARAH WALKER: Yes, it is. It's also the sort of thing where you can try to find some leniency in judgement. The situation that they are all in will affect different people in different ways.

MARK TYLER: Are you saying that this is entirely out of character for her?

SARAH WALKER: No, you've seen that she can be manipulative and aggressive already. I'm saying that the situation may have caused her to lash out more extremely than normal.[139]

MARK TYLER: And what about her desire to capture THe CreAturE and sell it? I believe she said, 'fuck the Guild', and 'let's go black market'?

SARAH WALKER: That…I can't defend it. I understand the want to catch and sell to a point. We're all mercenary here. But what else can we be? Big scores don't last forever.[140] You look at every opportunity presented to you and weigh them up. Here, she made what is in my opinion the wrong choice.

MARK TYLER: She threatened to shoot one of the salvage leads, too.

SARAH WALKER: Yes. She did. That is something that I will have to consider at length.

MARK TYLER: I would imagine it puts you in a tough position.

SARAH WALKER: It does, yes. I may be faced with the choice of losing her or losing Alex, Josh, Alice, and Stuart.[141]

MARK TYLER: If you don't mind me saying so, it seems like an obvious choice to me.

SARAH WALKER: That's because you're looking at this from a distance. These are all my colleagues. They're all my friends. I do not condone Lucy's actions, and the threatening behaviour breaks a number of rules. But I also know her. I have for years. I know what life she has led, and why she acts the way she does. I also know how she would react if I had to let her go. That makes this complicated.

MARK TYLER: Is there anything she could have done that would have made the decision easier?

SARAH WALKER: Other than not do it at all you mean?

[142] In a way, that would have made it harder. Lucy is stuck in a narrative and will need the others to work with her, even if reluctantly, to have the best chance of achieving her goal. Her killing one of them would be an indicator that she is no longer capable of changing their current thinking on it.

<While Lucy surviving is most important, this would still have been bad, as more facets changing their thinking on the creature would be a good sign that the subject can change their overall thinking in the long run and accept all parts of the act and subsequent consequences.>

MARK TYLER: [Nods]

SARAH WALKER: She could have pulled the trigger.[142]

MARK TYLER: Let's keep going.

[143] Because part of you is unsure how I feel about you right now. The "me" in the narrative was in favour of running. But you know that doing so would mean this can't change. So, Lucy is forcing me to go with her in an effort to shift the balance. To be clear, if I didn't want to try to save this, would I really be willing to break this many laws?

[144] Harsh. But potentially a sign that part of the problem is that you never really mourned the end of your relationship with him. You just kinda lay in it.

The crew exited the security office, filing out with Lucy at the back, the gun trained on them. Josh now had a Shock Glove, but it was Lucy that remained the best armed, with not only the gun and her own Shock Glove, but a suppression net launcher.

"The posh princess is with me," she said, beckoning Alex with the gun. Alex tensed. "Why?"[143]

"I'm pretty sure I could fly The Orca if I need to. There were only four licensed pilots on this salvage though, and you're the only one left." She nodded at Josh and added, "And I don't trust that one enough to work with him, or not to leave me here if I take Kemble. So, I'm eliminating that possibility. Give them the box. If this fails, we're at least taking that."

"Nice to know you intend to make it back, even if I don't," Alex said, handing Josh the box containing the flesh sample.

Josh glared at Lucy. "You say *you* don't trust me, but you don't seem too upset about Colt. I bet you saw one those things coming and used him as bait to save your own arse, didn't you?"

Lucy shrugged, her face neutral. "I just chose not to risk my life trying to save him. At the end of the day, he was just a big, scary-looking idiot. There are plenty more like him in every bar. Give me a week, I'll have a new Colt to do the heavy lifting. As long as I get my money after a salvage, the partner doesn't matter."

Josh screwed up his face in disgust, and Lucy laughed. "Aww, don't give me that look. Did I hit too close to home for you? This is why I don't trust you. We're too alike."

"I am *nothing* like you," Josh spat through gritted teeth.

"No?" Lucy tilted her head towards Alex. "You picked that one up soon enough after Macey died. Mourning is only for those who care, right?"[144]

Josh flexed the fingers on his Shock Glove and started to move towards Foster, but Alex shook their head and moved voluntarily to Foster's side. They sighed.

"Let's just get this over with."

Foster stepped behind Alex, using them as a shield and said, "Good. Now, you three go and find a way to get those doors open. Work quickly. Oh, and

[145] <While the dreams of being eaten relate to sex, the specific imagery here is also a symbol for the subject's cyclical thinking being self-destructive. They constantly relive the same issues and it all feeds into itself, allowing it to keep growing and, in turn, keep going.>

[146] <The Ego will often delay fulfilment in order to avoid negative consequences. Here, Lucy is taking it slow (and using logic) to avoid potential pain.>

Baby steps. But steps, nonetheless.

[147] My friend says that you've either slept with a lot of people since splitting up with him—and yes, I do understand that they were probably before you were with me—or this is an attempt to show you how much damage you're doing to yourself.

don't rely on that Shock Glove too much. Colt tried his on one of those things and it just made it angry."

Alex felt the pressure of Lucy's gun pressed into their back and let it guide them away from the others and towards the hatch to the second floor.

"What do you think they've been eating?" they asked.

"What?"

"THE CreAtures. Since all the people here died out, what do you think they've been eating?"

"What's the first meal that the babies eat when they're born?"[145]

Alex paused and looked down. "Oh." They checked the life sign scanner and said, "There are a lot more life signs dropping in and out on the map."

"The system is glitching, that's all. Watch the dots and assume they're accurate."

"I am. Look, the room where we keep seeing a lot of them? If the scan is right, then that's probably a nest."

Lucy sighed. "And your point is?"

"Two of us with one net, one gun, and one Shock Glove—all of which you're holding—against all of them? I don't like those odds. There's a room coming up on the right that's showing life signs too, but only two. That might be a better bet."

Lucy glanced at the map and nodded. "Okay, we'll try that one first."[146]

The door to the room that Alex spotted was open, its remains bent out of shape in the frame. It was a dance hall. Neon lights, only a few of which were still working, covered the floor, still flashing in a pre-programmed pattern as though in time with music. At the back of the room sat a DJ stage, with straps and a harness floating up from behind the desk. It was eerily silent.

"Look at the walls," Alex said. "The way they're smeared…the music must have attracted them, then the sound would have hit the blood and made it ripple off everywhere. But…they don't swallow people. So, where are the bodies?"

"Look up."

Alex turned to Foster, who was already staring upwards. They followed her gaze and the blood drained from their face. "That's…I can't tell what's clothing and what's shredded flesh. How many do you think there are?"[147]

"Who knows. Nothing I'm interested in though. If the system is still picking up false positives, there may not be that many in the apparent nest."

Alex tried to pull their gaze from the remains floating above them but couldn't. "Maybe."

[148] <The Ego sees the potential risk to dragging this out.>

Lucy, spotting Alex's lack of movement, nudged them back towards the door. "Come on. I don't want to stay here any longer than I have to."[148]

Stuart, Alice, and Josh made their way inside a small maintenance office. It was set out almost like the front-end of a hotel, with a single desk in the middle that stretched the length of the room. Behind the desk was a single door. Though closed, the power light was still on.

The crew pulled themselves over the desk and the automatic door release kicked in, causing the metal to slide aside with a quiet swoosh. Once inside, Alice called up her map and checked for life signs.

"All clear," she said.

Stuart glanced over the labels on a few shelves at the end of the first three sections of racking. "It looks like they used the same filing system as we did in my unit. The bigger tools should be this way."

Stuart moved on, and both Josh and Alice followed quietly. As they moved down the second to last aisle, Josh asked, "Did you ever hear about what happened here? In your unit, I mean?"

"I don't know. I would have still been a guest when it happened, so if we were told, I doubt any of us registered it."

Josh's eyes flicked over the labels, instinctively noting a few high value items. He shook the thoughts away and replied, "I still don't get why nobody came to collect the unit after the supply time limit ran out."

"I wasn't exactly high up the chain of command, so I couldn't say for sure. At a guess though?" Stuart shrugged. "Once they paid compensation to the families, they probably saw the biohazard classification and figured that it wasn't worth the trouble."

"I bet they have some hefty insurance on the units, too," Alice whispered.

"Probably. Okay, here we go." Stuart slid a drawer out and pulled out three identical items, handing two to Josh and one to Alice. He took a fourth from the drawer and held it up. It looked like a metal box with control panels on one side and two small crowbar heads flanked by holes on the other.

"Have you ever used one of these before?"

Alice and Josh both shook their heads, and Stuart explained, "They're called Door breakers. Basically, they're designed to deal with accidental lockdowns. The solid buttons run in order. Hit the red one first and the heads will heat up. Count to five, then push them hard against point where the doors

[149] This is a shift in attitude. It seems like they're still going with the running approach, but because of Lucy's actions, they're having to compromise. That's why the Door Breakers won't open the doors the whole way. They're there to crack the door open so that the facets can begin to deal with the issue. The problem is, that will hurt you, so there's still a fear there.

[150] He is the one best suited to the task. He is your hope to resolve the issues and this shift means he's heading back down that path.

meet. Get it tight against the door and press the orange button. Be careful. The moment you do, nails are going to come out of the holes, here. They'll lock it in place and the heads will start to cool. When the green button lights up, hit it and it'll start forcing the doors."

"Will that get them all the way open?" Josh asked.

"No. But if we alternate which side we put them on, they should break the locks. We can manually push the doors apart then."[149]

Alice cracked her neck. "Okay. Let's get this don—"

Click-click.

Click-click.

The crew froze in place. Slowly, Alice raised her Wrist Display and pulled up the map again. The life sign scanner showed a new blip, making its way down the aisle a few racks over. She nodded over her shoulder and the trio started to move.

As they turned the corner, one of Josh's Door Breakers caught on the corner of a rack, and the sound of metal scraping on metal rang out.

On Alice's map, the blip stopped and started moving back towards them. Panicking, they shoved off the wall and moved further into the room, away from the door. Once they found a set of large crates, they pulled themselves behind them, and hunkered down in silence until tHe CreATurE drifted past.

"It looks like it's patrolling," Alice said, keeping her voice low. "Now what do we do?"

Josh raised his hand, flashing the Shock Glove. "I'll try to sneak up on it. You two head back to the door and get it open."

Alice shook her head. "You heard Foster. The Glove won't kill it."

"It might slow it. Or maybe Colt was an idiot and it'll work just fine."

"Here it comes again," Stuart hissed, and they all dropped into silence again. Once THe CREATuRe has passed by, he said, "How about this. You two take the lock breakers, and I'll distract it."

"Are you insane?" Josh asked in disbelief. "Heroes don't live long, you know. And I can at least claim atonement."

"I know the layout of this place better than you two do. I know which doors should go where. If I get a little distance on it and draw its attention, I should be able to get it away from the hangar and double back."

Josh looked to Alice, and she gave him a brief, uncomfortable smile. "He is more familiar with the place than we are. It's probably the best shot we have."[150]

Without waiting for further discussion, Stuart handed his Door Breaker

to Alice and dragged himself over the crates. He moved to the main door and started banging out a steady rhythm on the door frame as he yelled, "Hey! Over here! Come and get me!"

A loud, angry barrage of *click-click-click* exploded out of the racking and Stuart stopped yelling, instead gliding out of the room. The door slid shut then, moment later, slid open and shut again.

After a few seconds of silence, Alice checked her map again. "Looks clear. Let's move."

Much like with the dance hall, the doors to the food hall were bent horribly out of shape. This time, they had been forced aside, leaving a diamond shaped gap for Alex and Lucy to pull themselves through.

Alex's map showed multiple life signs, but as the pair looked around, the room was devoid of life. Alex pointed upwards, grimacing at the mass of flesh and cloth floating above them. "The scanner must be picking up the dead crew and guests. There's nothing here, but...Let's just leave."

"No. Look at that."

Alex followed Lucy's pointing finger and frowned. "It doesn't look decayed like the others." Realization dawned on them, and they lifted a hand to cover their mouth as they squeaked, "Is that Rob?"

"Whether there are a hundred of these things, or just one, this is definitely a nest. It took him back here to eat later."

Clang.

Alex and Lucy's heads snapped around to face a room at the back of the hall.

"The kitchen?" Alex asked.

Lucy nodded and motioned them forward.

Alex swallowed hard and moved in front, quietly sliding the door aside.

Inside, one of tHe CrEATures writhed in the air, twisting and contorting as it crashed into hanging cutlery and trays. It scraped its quills together, creating a loud, spider-like hiss. It was in pain. Pure, primal pain. And all Alex and Lucy could do was watch in awe as its outer ring started to pulsate. Then, a noise rose above the hissing.

Riiiip.

The hissing slowed and died down as rivulets of blood spilled into the air, streaming out of a jagged slit in THE CreAture's outer ring. Thrashing and struggling against the torn flesh, a small, miniature version of tHe CREATurE pulled its way out. Immediately, it wrapped itself around part of its mother's carcass.

Soon, it was joined by three more, each with matching markings, and each hungrily clamped down on its dead progenitor. They moved independently of each other, and the tearing and slurping noises overlapped each other.

[151] <Identification with an Aggressor is a defence mechanism used by the Ego. It causes a person to meet aggression with aggression, for example. Here, rather than get eaten, Lucy has caught three of the babies by trapping them in a net. The way it wraps around them and locks them in place is similar to how the creatures wrap around their victims, too. That one escaped means part of the subject is still trying to engage flight rather than fight. If she had caught all four, this would be over now.>

That she caught most of them means she's still winning, though. That's a good thing.

[152] You made your bed, now lie in it. That's what my friend said. Ugh.

[153] I'm not actually angry about this. Your Ego is essentially trying to make it so that you concentrate on yourself rather than worrying about me and my reactions. That's needed, I think.

Slowly, Lucy pulled the suppression net launcher from her back and pointed it at the feeding children.

"Come on, you fucks," she mumbled.

Even as quiet as she was, her words seemed to reach the new-borns and they stopped feeding in unison. They all turned their quills towards the salvagers.

Click-click.

They all lunged forward.

Lucy pulled the trigger and the net launched forward, ensnaring three of the charging babies.[151] The moment the solid edges locked together, it sent a large electric shock along its strands, silencing THe CreATurEs instantly. The fourth child, having narrowly avoiding being caught, sped forward into the food hall, letting out a click-roar as it left the room.

Lucy pushed the launcher away and let it float across the room, having no further need for it now that the single-shot ammo had been used up. She grabbed the net and tied it to her back, wearing it like a backpack.

"Three will do," she said. "Let's—"

Another click-roar sounded, cutting her words short. It came in louder than that of the baby.

Then, another responded.

And another.

And another.

Quickly, the voices built up, until the room was full of discordant clicks and hisses. Alex and Foster exited the kitchen and looked up.

Alex gasped, horrified. Above them, creatures were pushing out from above the half-shredded remains of the crew. They writhed and twisted in the air as they tried to track Alex and Lucy with their quills. Realization set in. "They didn't hear us when we came in because they were asleep…they were using the crew as bedding."[152]

Lucy didn't respond. She just started moving at speed towards the door.

Alex followed and they both picked up speed, manoeuvring through the halls, with a loud run of clicks following somewhere behind. "We need to find a way to slow them down," Alex said.

"Agreed. I'd love to say I'm sorry."

Lucy twisted in the air and grabbed Alex, yanking them around and trying to force them back towards the food hall.

"What are you doing?" Alex shrieked, grabbing Lucy's wrists and trying to stop her attack.

They crashed against a wall and spun into a small, ransacked room. Lucy

[154] She may be on the run, but Lucy is still fighting.

shoved Alex away, sending them crashing into a table. Looking to end things, Lucy pushed herself toward Alex, her Shock Glove raised. Alex scrambled backwards, barely avoiding the blast as they tumbled into the next room.

"I'm getting out of here. You're going to keep them busy for me,"[153] Lucy roared, following Alex. Once inside, she looked left to right and frowned, "Where did—"

An angry ring of quills barrelled into Lucy, slicing the strap on her Wrist Display as it wrapped itself around her.

"No," Lucy hissed, slamming her hands and feet out against the inner edges of its body, trying to force the quills back and prevent it from completely engulfing her. Again, she activated the Shock Glove, and let out a full-strength blast, causing tHE CreATure to release her.

Wincing in pain, Lucy pushed off the wall, and out the next door. Moments later, THe burnt CREATurE gave chase.[154]

Part of the wall rippled as Alex deactivated their camouflage, cutting the cameras on their Skin Suit. Breathing rapidly, they checked their map and started to move.

[155] This is not literal, of course, but it does have a clear analogue. You're worried that bringing everything out and dealing with it directly would end our relationship. As it's Lucy that's aiming for that course of action, she is in essence attempting to murder the relationship. In reality, I'd view her as trying to save it. But you have no way of knowing that in the Sim.

[156] Cold, but true, Josh.

MARK TYLER: At this point, it should be clear that Lucy Foster is charge-able with attempted murder.[155]

SARAH WALKER: Yes.

MARK TYLER: You don't agree with that decision, do you?

SARAH WALKER: Actually, I do. The law is the law, and her actions are irrefutable.

MARK TYLER: But?

SARAH WALKER: [Shakes her head] There is no but. Not now. All I can do for her is to try to explain why she makes the decisions she does. There are only so many things that can be excused though. In the end, we all have to take responsibility for our choices, no matter the reasoning.[156]

MARK TYLER: On that, we definitely agree.

SARAH WALKER: I need to know. Were there any shots of the bodies? Either in the dance floor or the food hall?

MARK TYLER: No. I think we can both be thankful for that.

SARAH WALKER: [Silence]

MARK TYLER: Do you agree with Stuart's decision to act as bait?

SARAH WALKER: [Sighs] I don't know. Based on pure logic, he was right. He knows the layout better than either Josh or Alice. At the same time though, I'd have rather they found a way to get out of there without any of them playing potential sacrifice.

MARK TYLER: Which appears to be exactly what Josh wanted to put himself up as. He described it as 'atonement.'

SARAH WALKER: He has nothing to atone for.

[157] This, I'm sure, is literal.

[158] Deeper than you realized? Or was it that you didn't want to accept what was festering?

[159] I certainly got the impression that you loved him. And that part of you still did.

[160] The problem is, you listened to all the bad stuff and took it to mean that your own self-criticisms were right.

[161] 'To a point' is an important statement. It has that duality again. You hid the way you felt to a point, but you couldn't hide all of it from yourself. You can only shove so many things to the back of your head. And, you hid what you were up to, but only to a point. Which brings it all back to the event being ticketed. And kinda makes me think that maybe I should come off the Neg-Vacs. Are they really all that healthy when, mostly, this is what they do too? Like, are we being forced into unhealthy methods of coping because they make us easier to control? Maybe your paranoia is rubbing off on me.

[162] You blamed yourself 'at first.' Which means part of you accepted that it wasn't all your fault.

MARK TYLER: Clearly, he feels differently. From what you've said already, it sounds like he's not the only one either.

SARAH WALKER: That's not…No. No, you're right. And that's my fault to a degree. This was my way to try to get things back on track for Josh. In terms of colleague relationships, I mean. The problem is, I should have dealt with how prevailing that viewpoint is long before now.

MARK TYLER: You said earlier that, and I quote, 'you made damn sure that the rest of the Guild knew what the official ruling was. That doesn't stop them thinking it though.' That sounds to me like you did try to deal with the issue, and that it was simply not easy to rectify?[157]

SARAH WALKER: [Takes a deep breath, holds it, and releases] I dealt with it to the minimum level required by the rules of the Guild. Looking at…all of this, the whole thing has had a deeper effect on Josh than I realized.[158]

MARK TYLER: That's…interesting. Did you not think that he would be hurt by the accusations, especially after being cleared of wrong doing?

SARAH WALKER: Hurt, yes. But we all were. Macey was a well-respected and much-loved member of the Guild.[159] I thought that Josh knew that he wasn't truly to blame and that, even if cut when people said things, it wouldn't scar.[160]

MARK TYLER: Is there a reason you didn't consider that he may have felt differently? Did he hide it, for example?

SARAH WALKER: I suppose he did, to a point.[161] Mostly though, I was trying to justify the actions of others. Things with no justification, I deal with. Quickly, and harshly. When I can see a reason for someone to behave poorly, I'm more forgiving. When it came to what happened to Macey, I could understand why people were angry. I was angry too. And I blamed Josh, too, at first.[162]

MARK TYLER: So, you let some things slide?

SARAH WALKER: Because I could see why the people felt the way they did. We all needed to mourn. I think I convinced myself that,

[163] This is good, Josh. You're beginning to see where you've miss-stepped in how you dealt with this.

[164] The voices of those around you made you feel like you really were the bad guy, didn't they? And then you began to really believe it. Like Sarah, I should have done more to stop that. Shit.

[165] Yes! Keep going with this.

given time, people would work through it and realize that they were wrong.[163]

MARK TYLER: Repeated exposure to false information increases the tendency to believe said information. It's called the illusory truth effect. In this case, the Guild members probably created a pseudo echo chamber too, increasing the exposure even more.[164]

SARAH WALKER: No, I created that. Inadvertently. I will find a way to fix that.

MARK TYLER: Do you think that this line of thinking, seeking justification for others' actions, accounts for your reluctance to see the bad in Lucy Foster?

SARAH WALKER: [Flinches] It was less not seeing the bad, and more not accepting that it was simply that, but yes.

MARK TYLER: Has the footage, and our discussions for that matter, affected your view of any members of the team?

SARAH WALKER: Yes.

MARK TYLER: Talking hypothetically here, but if Josh had been the decoy and it had resulted in his death, would it had been seen as atonement by his colleagues?

SARAH WALKER: For those that don't believe he was in the wrong, obviously not. For some, yes though. Others, no. It might have depended on who they viewed him as saving. Alice, may be. Lucy, maybe, in some groups. Alex, no.

MARK TYLER: Is Alex that hated?

SARAH WALKER: Not as much as Josh. Those that don't have so much of an issue with them usually don't view Josh as to blame for Macey's death though. At the very least, not enough to think he needs to *atone*.

MARK TYLER: I suppose that, in a way, it wouldn't make a measurable difference overall. Guilt on the whole is self-imposed. The views of others cement it for you, or in some cases, increase it. But that initial guilt always comes from inside.[165]

SARAH WALKER: You sound like you have some experience in that.

[166] I still feel like this relates to us. You know you'll have to face the consequences of this eventually. I will too.

MARK TYLER: We all do, I'm sure.

SARAH WALKER: Yes, but this feels recent. Raw. It has something to do with your husband, doesn't it? You've mentioned him and how you viewed his work a few times now. And you're always sad. What role do you think you played in his death?

MARK TYLER: That I will have to face eventually. But that's not the point right now.[166] Do feel ready to continue with the review?

SARAH WALKER: [Stares at Mark, then nods and waves in the affirmative]

FILE NAME: RECORDING TWENTY – THE ORCA, INTERNAL MONITORING SYSTEM
FILE REFERENCE: 43757587990065120501192029790O
TRANSCRIBED BY: █████ , █████ █████████

In the hangar, Josh and Alice rushed towards the inner doors blocking The Orca. They both hit the first button on one Door Breaker, counted down, and slammed it against the door and hit the second button. Then, they repeated the process again. Once all four green lights were lit, they pressed the final buttons, and the doors were forced apart.

They squeezed inside the newly made gap and started moving through The Orca, powering up systems as they went. Josh hit the comms button on their Wrist Display and asked, "Alex, Foster. Any update?"

"I'm on my way," Alex replied. "So are THe CreATurEs. Have you got the doors open?"

"Just about. And tHE CreATuREs? Plural?"

"Yeah. They weren't false positives."

"Where's Foster?" Alice asked.

"Dead, I think. Fuck her. I'll get there as quick as I can."

"What about Stuart?" Alice asked.

Josh nodded. "Stuart? Are you still out there?"

There was a moment of silence, then Stuart replied, "I keep getting boxed in. I can't—Shit! How many of them are there? Wait. Okay, yeah. I'm heading to the control room. Get ready to disengage."

Josh frowned. "What about you?"

"Don't worry. I have a plan."

"Damn it. Alex. How close are you?"

"I don't know. There are so many of these things, I—" Alex's voice cut to silence.

Josh paused. "Alex? Alex, respond! Fuck!" Panicking, Josh started rifling through boxes, only stopping when he found a knife. "That'll have to do."

Alice, noticing Josh moving back towards the door grabbed him by the shoulder. "What are you doing?"

"Alex is the last pilot left."

"I know, but—"

"I'm not leaving them behind," Josh cut in.

Alice shook her head. "Look. What Foster said about not trusting you not to leave her behind?"

[167] I discussed this at length with my friend. I think that, as atonement is being presented as death for this Josh, it represents simply falling on your sword and just accepting that you are what you, and others, seem to think you are. Alice is beginning to turn and try to get you to accept a fate other than simply being that.

[168] I love you too Josh. That's why this all hurts so much.

[169] I questioned this revelation and how it related to the idea that Macey's death was representative of you splitting up with him. What my friend said actually kinda made sense. He was bad for you and, in a way, his actions led to you growing some bad habits. Sure, they grew and changed by your own hand, but in a way, he birthed this version of you. In that regard, he is the mother of some of your worst traits.

[170] Is this you accepting that you need to reach out for help?

[171] The guilt is creeping in again, but it's not trying to kill you. You're coming up with plans.

Josh pushed her away. "Don't."

"I was on the peer review team for the St. Michael incident. There was nothing you could have done to save Macey. You don't need to prove anything. You don't need any atonement.[167] So quit being an idiot."

"I love Alex![168] Since Macey…Mum[169]…Alex is the only family I have left. Wouldn't you have saved Rob if you could have?" Alice flinched and Josh looked away, the guilt etched on his face. "I'm sorry. Just…if we don't make it back, you should be able to cut the ship loose and radio for help. They'll help you set up the autopilot."[170]

Alice sighed and nodded. She turned away as he left the bridge and started powering up the main controls. Once everything was on, she stopped, and a smile crept onto her face. Her fingers flew over the keyboard as she synched the life sign scanner up with The Orca's screen and searched for a specific setting.

"Got you," she said.

Behind her, a strange shape floated upwards, nestling in above the low hanging cables.[171]

[172] You know that WE have to talk eventually if this is going to be resolved.

[173] When you talk about it, the guilt doesn't grow. It doesn't kill. It stops so that it can be dealt with.

Now back in the first-floor residential area, Alex moved quickly between rooms. They made use of their environment to pick up speed, intermittently activating and deactivating their Mag Boots to shove large, free floating items back towards THE advancing CreAtures.

They pushed off walls, turning and twisting through gaps, suddenly grateful for the Josh's insistence that they should try microgravity parkour.

As Alex turned a corner, their eyes went wide. One of tHe CrEATures had somehow gotten ahead of them and was speeding out of a door just ahead.

Before it could reach them, the door slid shut, and Alice's voice came through the unit speakers. "Keep moving, Alex. I'm shutting what doors I can, but the downside to blocking them off is that they'll be funneled towards you eventually."[172]

"Got it."

"Wait, here's a thought." Alice paused, and when her voice came back, it was louder. "How's this, you fuckers?"

Alex frowned. "What the..."

"Ha! They can feel the vibrations from the speakers! Every time I talk, they slow and stick in place.[173] I think it's confusing them!"

A relieved smile grew on Alex's face. "Then keep going!"

"You don't need to tell me twice. You should be coming to the hangar in a moment. Shit! The door won't close. Alex, look out!"

"Wha—"

Alex was slammed against the wall by THe CreAturE that sped through the door to their left. They managed to slip out from its grip but tore their Skin Suit in the process. A sharp pain hit them, and they cried out, realizing that their arm had been cut too.

"Josh, get back to the main door!" Alice yelled, but tHe CrEATuRE was too intent on Alex to become distracted.

Alex tried to wriggle free, but their arm was growing cold and numb. Finally, THE CreAture managed to clamp down over Alex and lock them against the wall. Alex didn't scream. They just closed their eyes and waited.

Then, the light came back, and Josh was there. He forced tHE CreATure away from Alex and pressed it against the wall, keeping its back facing him. He

[174] I hope this is the obvious: You're fighting. For us.

[175] This is a very good sign. You didn't kill the creature. You stopped it in place, yes, but you didn't kill it. To save me. You're moving slowly in the right direction. If this ends the way it's looking, we will have a lot to talk about. We'll both have apologies to make. I accept that. But we can work together. We can make 'us' work.

blasted it with the Shock Glove, trying to keep a grip on it as it roared in anger. Unrelenting, and desperate,[174] Josh pressed his feet against a nearby crate and activated his Mag Boots. Then, he swung the knife.

Josh slashed and cut THE CREATure's back, stabbing upwards to try to get through to the inner ring. Finally, with a guttural scream, he slammed the knife through its back, impaling it against the wall.

With tHe CreATurE hissing and wriggling next to him, Josh turned to Alex and offered his hand.[175]

Alex took it, pulled Josh close, and kissed him. They breathed in Josh's scent, desperately clinging to him as they tried to calm down. When they finally pulled away, Josh simply smiled, disengaged his Mag Boots, and led them back to The Orca.

Once inside the bridge, Alice turned to greet them, a relieved look on her face. "Thank fuck for that. Still no Stuart though."

Josh nodded and raised his Wrist Display. "Stuart? Where are you?"

[176] <Stuart is showing enough insight here to have begun to understand the nature of the creatures, but he's uncertain. That's why he still wants to kill them. This is symptomatic of fear relating to taking that final step.>

In the control room, Stuart was already working on a computer. To his relief, the systems he wanted were still active.

Bang. Bang. Bang.

He briefly glanced up at the only door into the room, checking that it was still shut and that the locked light was still on, glowing in the darkness.

"Stuart? Where are you?" Josh's voice came through his Wrist Display.

"I'm in the control room."

"Alice has control of the doors, and she's been using sound to distract tHe CrEATuREs. Tell us where it is, and we'll try to get you out."

Stuart shook his head, concentrating on the screen. "Don't. Just disengage The Orca."

"What about you?" Alex asked.

"I told you, I have a plan. I'm going to shut down the oxygen flow and suffocate them."

"Again, what about you? And how do you know that'll even work?"

Stuart bit his lip, not truly certain. Still, he replied, "The system has been pumping oxygen in all this time, right? Even if Dr. Michalas hadn't confirmed it on the video, the system reads usage and adjusts levels appropriately. They have to be breathing it, they just don't need as much of it as we do. If I cut it, they'll die. Eventually.[176] Hopefully quicker than one of us would."

Behind Stuart, a shape rose out of the shadows, completely hidden by the lack of a working light. Unaware, he continued, "And don't worry about me. When the biohazard classification was set, the escape pods were locked down. Now that the time limit has passed, they're open again. It looks like there's only one that isn't damaged, but it should get me off the unit. You just make sure you pick me up."

Alex paused then said, "Okay. Disengaging now. Make sure you get out here quick. We lost Foster. I don't want to lose you, too."

The loud clang of The Orca disengaging echoed through the unit, and for a moment, the banging on the door subsided. Soon enough, it started up again.

"Ten minutes should be enough time," Stuart mumbled.

Cla-click.

Stuart's eyes went wide. He turned to see Lucy Foster facing him, her gun

[177] This ties in with the last note. Now that he understands things better, he's afraid of what it will mean to take them into The Orca.

[178] <This isn't really backing down as she's still certain she can fit them in.>

[179] <The Ego is making sure there is no further opposition to its goal. It's harsh, but she's essentially eliminating fear.>

aimed at his face. "Forgetting someone?" she asked.

"Foster? We thought you were dead!" He nodded at the net hanging over her shoulder. "Did you…?"

"Three babies. Noisy fuckers. They're smart, though. A few shocks every time they made that annoying clicking and they soon shut up."

Stuart recoiled, aghast. "You can't still want to take them off the unit!"[177]

"Can't I? See, these things are going to make me a fortune. In fact, I'm certain I want to take *them* with me. *You?* Not so much, given you're planning to suffocate me along with them."

"I didn't know you were still alive!" he pleaded. "Look. Look at the screen. The escape pods. See? There's only one working one left. AUScarlet. They're only meant to be for one person, but we should both be able to squeeze in until we're picked up. You…you'll need to leave the net behind though."

"Like fuck, I will!" Lucy growled, the words rumbling from her throat like a lion.

"I'm being serious! We won't both fit otherwise. Look, the pods are just down the hall to the right. You'll see when we get there."

Lucy paused, thinking it through, then nodded. "Okay, if we get there and we don't all fit, I'll leave the net.[178] If you're lying though?" She waved the gun at him, then put it back in her Skin Suit pocket. "Now let me ask you this. You hear that banging at the door? There's got to be at least ten of them out there. How the fuck are we going to get past them?"

Stuart smiled. "I already thought of that. They hunt by reading changes in the air. From what Josh said, sound should draw them in. I'm turning the music on in the dance hall."

Stuart tapped some keys and a bass beat started to build in the background. Slowly, the noise at the door subsided. Stuart checked the map on his Wrist Display, and Lucy leant over to check too.

"Looks like the halls are clear. For now." She tapped a point on the map. "That's where we're heading, right?"

"Right."

Without hesitation, Lucy drew the gun and shot Stuart in the head. She waited, watching his lifeless body rise upward with a growing string of blood. When no sound came back to the door, she smiled and removed his Wrist Display. "Guess I won't have to leave the net after all."[179]

Lucy moved out into the hallway and started heading for the escape pods. She called up the comms and said, "This is Foster. I'm heading to the escape pod now."

[180] <In a way, she has assumed the role of understanding here. She has taken Stuart's spot as a representation of hope.>

[181] I'm fighting back tears, Josh. Lucy surviving and getting a creature off the unit was the best scenario. I just hope the one that snuck on board the ship survives. Maybe these are just babies because they're the potential for future problems, and them getting left behind means they won't happen. Maybe the one of the ship is now solely representative of what happened. I'm reaching. I know I am. You're losing the fight, Josh. Please. Don't give in.

"Foster?" Josh asked. "Where's Stuart? This is reading as his communicator."[180]

"Yeah, well, I can't use mine, because someone left me for dead, and it got broken."

"You tried to sacrifice me to save yourself, remember?" Alex replied. "Where's Stuart?"

"He didn't make it. I got to the control room just after you disengaged. He set off the dance hall music to lure THe CrEAtures away from us. We were going to share a pod, but one of tHE CReATurEs found us. It must have been slower than the others or something. It caught him before either of us could do anything."

Lucy pressed the door release button and the escape pod door slid open. "I'm about to enter the pod now."

Before she could float inside, a small shape drifted down from the ceiling in front of her. It took her less than a second to recognize it as tHE baby CreATure that had escaped earlier.

It took THE CReATurE less than a second to dart forward and wrap itself around her head.

Lucy screamed and fell inside the pod, kicking her feet violently and trying to rip THe CrEAture off her. The suppression net slipped off her back and fell open, releasing the other three babies.[181]

[182] I had hoped this wouldn't happen. There is still some hope though.

[183] And this is why. You're understanding that your actions were wrong and that, even if you justify them, it still hurt someone else.

In the bridge, the remaining salvagers listened as Lucy screamed over the comms. Then, the sound cut.

"Foster. Are you there?" Alex asked.

Silence.

"Foster?"

Silence.[182]

Alex sighed and called up the comms system on the ship's controls, setting up an emergency broadcast. "Salvagers Guild Three HQ," they said, "this is The Orca, stationed by reference twenty-seventeen, alpha-three. The Ailuros unit…there was a problem. We're heading back now. Surviving crew, Alex Holden, Joshua Byrne, and Alice Kemble."

Alex turned back to Josh and Alice and added, "I've deployed the scent markers and set the ship to autopilot. I'm going to go and get a drink while we wait for Sarah to respond to the message."

"I'll be with you in a minute," Josh replied. Alex nodded and floated quietly from the room, their shoulders slumped. Once they were gone, Josh turned to Alice. "I really am sorry. What I said about your brother wasn't right. I was worried. About Alex."

"I know." She let out a frustrated grunt. "It still hurt though."[183]

Alice turned away, and neither she nor Josh saw THe CrEAtuRE descend from the cabling.

"We should probably—" Josh began, but his words turned to a scream as tHE CreATure slammed its quills into his shoulder. The scream choked out, and Josh paled as he tried to turn, but the pain only intensified as THE CreATurE dug its quills in deeper.

Without warning, it started to whip itself from side to side, shaking Josh, and spreading blood throughout the room.

Now seeing what was happening, Alice dove forward and tried to pull THE CreAture off Josh. She managed to force a small corner of its body up, pulling the quills out of Josh's arm, but froze.

There, stuck between its quills was a finger wearing a small, silver tribal band.

"Rob…" she whispered, and her eyes glazed over. Slowly, she reached

[184] You framed this as a good thing. You made Alice the hero, gaining revenge for her brother's death. But without a surviving monster, you're simply hiding, Josh.

[185] But still fighting. The creature made it onto The Orca. That was important. That means you know what you're dealing with. How this ends for Sarah and Mark is what matters now.

up and grabbed one of the low hanging cables. Without pause, she pulled on it, and ripped it free, sending sparks flying. She jammed the end into tHe CreATurE's back.

THe CrEAture yanked back and clattered its quills together in a shriek.

The cable flashed and a small explosion cut all other sound.

THE CreAture was now silent and unmoving, its back burnt.[184]

Alice shook her head, waking herself up, and moved quickly to the control panel. She shut down the power cable just as Alex sped into the room.

"How did…Josh! What happened?"

Alice floated over and checked his pulse. "He's alive. We need to get him to the medical bay."

Alex nodded mutely and the two slowly, carefully moved Josh from the room.

Shortly after they left, tHE CReATurE's outer ring started to pulsate.[185]

[186] That would mean no internal exploration, just slaying the creatures without facing up to what they mean.

[187] Your unconscious is hurting and wants to just destroy everything without finishing the battle.

SARAH WALKER: [Stands up, fists clenched] Nobody told me that a creature made it onto The Orca. Why didn't you mention it after you let me see the damn things?

MARK TYLER: We couldn't. Not immediately. As far as we're aware, tHE CreATurE only gave birth to three, not four, babies.

SARAH WALKER: They've been stranded on the ship for three days! Are they all still alive?

MARK TYLER: Yes. Comms are still operational, at least in some rooms, and we've kept in regular contact since.

SARAH WALKER: Then why haven't you done something to get them out of there?

MARK TYLER: The risks involved with—

SARAH WALKER: —Fuck the risks! Someone should be trying to save them! If I'd known, I wouldn't be here waiting, I'd have been trying to get on board The Orca.

MARK TYLER: Which is why we couldn't tell you. We needed to speak to you about the case before doing anything else.[186]

SARAH WALKER: Anything else. So does that mean that you're going to get in there? Armed, I assume?

MARK TYLER: I put that case forward. [Shakes head] Unfortunately, my request was rejected. The heads in charge of the case deemed tHe CrEATures too dangerous to tackle. They'll deal with it, but...

SARAH WALKER: But what?

MARK TYLER: They intend to blow the ship up.[187]

SARAH WALKER: [Drops into her seat, shocked]

MARK TYLER: I'm sorry.

[188] Sarah is technically on a mission that could still result in killing the creatures, but it's primarily a rescue. My friend said that that may work out the same as if Lucy had survived. If Sarah gets the others out and leaves the creatures alive, it means that she fully assimilated Lucy's thinking on this.

SARAH WALKER: You're sorry? Fuck you.

MARK TYLER: I assume discussing this further is out of the question?

SARAH WALKER: You assume correctly.

MARK TYLER: Okay. [Stands up] For what it's worth, the paperwork required to take the actions planned takes a minimum of twenty-four hours to clear. The case leads only started the process today. Technically speaking, as Director of Salvagers Guild Three, until the paperwork clears, The Orca is classed as your property. Which means that you—and anyone else you wish to invite—can enter the ship as and when you wish.

SARAH WALKER: [Stands up and starts to leave but stops and turns back to Mark Tyler] Thank you.

MARK TYLER: Bring fire. If there's one thing we learned from my husband's final transmission…they burn.[188]

SARAH WALKER: [Nods and leaves]

[189] That is the point here, isn't it? Some things can be forgiven in some circumstances. Others cannot.

[190] In a way, this, too, is the point. I need to know what happened.

[191] This is a confirmation that something has happened ten times. Given what the creatures represent, I think we know what it is, don't we?

[192] I was happy to see this though. When taken as a whole, this sentence shows that you understand the damage you're doing. That it's hard to watch means it's hard for you think about.

[193] If the idea of suffering the same thing seems that bad to you, why do it, Josh? You clearly know the hurt it's causing.

[194] My friend said this is a positive. Self-judgement is important, and you're focussing on how it affects me. That shows you care.

[195] You're planning to confess it all. Please let that be the case.

In the case of Ailuros Unit Twenty-Three, the overall findings are complex in nature. Granted, there are some undeniable facts. Alice Kemble for example, did not break any major protocol during the mission, whereas Lucy Foster committed several highly chargeable offenses. Variance occurs between acts that are normally chargeable and the potential for a reasonable excuse for actions when you consider the deeper issues at play here.[189] Even Lucy can be forgiven some transgressions when this is taken into consideration.

'Heroes don't live long,' Josh Byre said. In truth, the reality is that none of us do in the grand scheme of things. Maybe the events on board the unit hammered that fact home for salvagers, even if only subconsciously.[190] The truth is, this was never going to be a simple open and shut case. Harrowing is a word that I have used when running through the video clips. Even upon the tenth viewing,[191] it is no easier to watch, or to imagine the way those involved must have felt.[192]

Loss. Of course, that is the easiest part to understand. Can we really place ourselves sufficiently in the mind of the victims to cast a fair judgement here, though? A video clip. Transcriptions of conversations. In truth, these are not enough to fully appreciate what they must have felt. Only being there would allow that, and would any of us truly want that? No.[193]

I feel, however, that I have a complete enough understanding of the events to make certain recommendations. Moreover, I would like to make it clear that in this instance, I do not feel that variance from my recommendations *can* ever be justified.

Such is this case that to act on anything other than the absolutely undeniable would be a breach in human decency. Of course, to a point, this only applies to how we will judge ourselves on our choices in relation to the survivors.[194] Ratifying any charges here would be potentially frowned upon were the case to reach public hands.

Really, that must be inevitable though. You know as well as I do that some things simply cannot be kept silent forever.[195]

Sarah Walker shouldn't be touched by the way. Even after entering The Orca. After killing tHe CreATurEs. Really, she's a hero, even if only to her own crew. Check back through the file. Her actions would be cleared as legal in any court of law. For starters, the law I stated was correct, meaning she had

[196] I'm numb. You were so close, Josh. That you accept that real life is hard is good, don't get me wrong, but this all points to one thing. You simply aren't ready to deal with your issues. You may well never be.

I had really hoped that this would end differently. It's my fault, in part. And I know I screwed up in how I dealt with it. If you feel the need to call the police, do so. I deserve that. I just wish that I could have seen more positives to take from this. All I really know now is that you absolutely did do something that I would define as cheating, that it may have happened more than once, and that you aren't in a place where we can fix this.

I'm sorry, Josh.

But this is goodbye.

Take care, lover.

justification to act if she believed herself that the ship was not yet claimed. Or if someone in a perceived position of power convinced her of the same.

Really, you don't have a chance at charging her. My personal opinion is that you shouldn't charge her. Or any of the others. Reality is tough at the best of times. Even more so when faced with what they were.[196]

SARAH WALKER

- *Professional Negligence:* I recommend no charge is raised. The grounds for this charge would be reliant on two points. One, that her choice of team members was unduly affected by her personal circumstances and two, that she did not work to ensure that the salvage was safe. Her justification for the choice of team members is reasonable, negating point one. Though she did admit that monetary gain came into her decision to approve the job, she acted on the information held, specifically the assurances given by Thornton-Hythe. Without a clear warning of specific danger, this was reasonable on her part.

- *Negligent Manslaughter:* As per the above, negligence does not apply in this instance. As such, the removal of the initial charge would result in the removal of this one.

- *Unlawful Entry:* I recommend no charge is raised. While The Orca was claimed under UNID Hostile Environments Act s6p3b, Sarah Walker was not aware of this. The events on board The Orca transpired due to my advice. I was careful to include that portion of our conversation in the core file, as I wanted to ensure that she had a reasonable excuse for her actions. Frankly, that she was able—with the assistance of only one other, who I see she is guarding in terms of identity—to rescue the survivors deserves praise. Even if only for her own colleagues, she is a hero.

ALEX HOLDEN

- *Attempted Murder:* I recommend no charge is raised. The basis of this charge is that they intentionally acted in such a way that would potentially result in the death of Lucy Foster. Thought this is technically true, Lucy's actions leading up to the event were more overtly in line with this charge. Alex's actions were not even strong enough to be classed as self-defence, so to raise this charge would be ridiculous.

- *Professional Negligence:* I recommend no charge is raised. As part of the leadership team for the salvage, it was Alex's duty to ensure the safety of their team. Throughout the events, the only time that they did not act in such a way as to work towards this aim was when members of the team intentionally disobeyed commands and/or obstructed their wishes. There is no basis for this charge

- *Unprofessional Conduct:* I recommend that no charge is raised. Alex generally kept their attitude in check throughout and only rose above necessary sternness once. This came when they believed Lucy Foster to be dead and the anger shown was proportionate to Lucy's actions and the stress of the situation they were in.

- *Theft:* I recommend that no charge is raised. While Alex is the last to have held the USB stick from Dr. Michalas, it is not inconceivable that it was lost during the events that followed its retrieval. We are unsure if there are more files on the stick than we saw in the footage retrieved from The Orca. So, we cannot be sure that theft applies.

JOSH BYRNE

- *Animal Cruelty:* I recommend no charge is raised. Technically speaking, Josh is guilty of harming a living creature. We neither know THe CREAtuRE's origin or the numbers in respect of their overall population, meaning we could theoretically be dealing with an endangered species. However, multiple cases have arisen on Earth whereby a person has killed an animal, not due to criminal cruelty, but to save their own life. This applies in this case.

- *Professional Negligence:* I recommend no charge is raised. As part of the leadership team for the salvage, it was Josh's duty to ensure the safety of his team. Throughout the events on board the unit, his actions were dictated by what was occurring around him.

- *Unprofessional Conduct:* I recommend that a minor charge is raised. I would love to say that he was justified at all times, but certainly his behaviour prior to the meeting with Sarah Walker was questionable. Tone is important, as is content. He did not attempt to de-escalate the situation, but rather to simply shift where it would happen. Witness accounts also confirm that he was ready to fight. He also stated himself that he would fight fire with more fire. He is not the only guilty party, however, and his actions did not extend far enough to warrant a full reprimand. A warning should suffice.

ROB KEMBLE, DECEASED

- No charges considered.

ALICE KEMBLE

- *Unprofessional Conduct:* I recommend that a minor charge is raised. Her actions in the hangar certainly amount to unprofessional, and she would likely have fully understood that they would make the conflict worse. This is not enough to warrant a full reprimand, however, and a warning should suffice.

- ***Criminal Damage:*** I recommend that no charge is raised. While it is true that she did pull a power cable during the events shortly after disengagement from the unit, this was due to the requirement to defend the life of herself and her crewmates. Under the circumstances, this was reasonable.

- ***Animal Cruelty:*** I recommend no charge is raised. Much as with Josh Byrne, Alice is guilty of harming a living creature. In her case, killing one. However, the same thinking applies here. This was a case of self defence.

- ***Theft:*** I recommend that no charge is raised. The charge relates to missing computer files, retrieved during the events on board the unit. While it is true that Alice is the crew member with the most technical knowledge, and so the most likely to have taken the files, there is no evidence to link their removal to her. Analysis shows that they were removed remotely.

KEVIN STOCKLEY, DECEASED

- No charges considered.

STUART GRANT, DECEASED

- No charges considered.

AARON COLT, DECEASED

- ***Unprofessional Conduct:*** I recommend that a charge is raised on three counts. In terms of general conduct, Aaron Colt was an aggressive member of the team. He was certainly unprofessional in the way he dealt with both Alex Holden and Josh Byrne. Witnesses also confirm that he made the initial confrontation with Josh Byrne physical. On the point of relationship with leadership, he was guilty of not waiting for orders, or following the requests of the salvage leads. Finally, he was also guilty of acting in a manner that endangered his crewmates. By lying about weapon stocks, and also ensuring that there was nothing on hand for the rest of the team, Colt ensured that danger could not be minimized. Even if he truly believed that there was no real danger, this was reckless, and warrants a full charge. I believe that a fine should be calculated and claimed via his estate.

- ***Theft:*** I recommend that no charge is raised. He certainly attempted to steal sal-vage, but failed in his attempts. I do, however, recommend that a further investigation be opened by the Guild in relation to the indication that he had done so before.

[197] This is the summary of my final findings in the case of Alex Holden [Genderfluid AMAB, 30] and Josh Byrne [Male AMAB, 31].

As you are aware, the Neg-Vac/Alleviation Sim [NVAS] works via a joint system. The regular injections use a mix of chemicals, custom built for each user, to supress brain functions related to specific negative emotional reactions, often cited as justification for criminal activity. This treatment is then accompanied by a mandated monthly VR Simulation where the supressed emotions are released in a controlled virtual environment. These are then studied for signs of degradation in behavioural patterns and signs of potential future offenses.

Of course, over time, the human body adapts to stimuli. As such, this monitoring is incredibly important as it allows use to tweak each user's experience as needed. Sometimes though, it isn't able to catch everything. For example, when an event occurs that causes such a strong reaction that the user's normal dosage won't fully supress it, it creates the potential for extreme behavioural shifts. Such is the case here.

LUCY FOSTER, DECEASED

- ***Unprofessional Conduct:*** I recommend that a charge is raised on one count. While I suspect that she was pulling the strings in relation to Aaron Colt's behaviour, this cannot be proven. She was certainly party to the situation relating to the crew's weapon stores though. As such, as with Aaron Colt, her behaviour put the crew in danger. I believe that a fine should be calculated and claimed via her estate.

- ***Theft:*** I recommend that no charge is raised. It could be argued that she stole the gun, but under the circumstances, it could equally be argued that she simply did not have opportunity to note it down. As with Aaron Colt, she failed to steal salvage, but the indication that she has done so before warrants a recommendation for a further investigation be opened by the Guild.

- ***Threatening Behaviour:*** I recommend that a charge be raised. She made several direct threats to her crew mates. This is irrefutable. I believe that a fine should be calculated and claimed via her estate.

- ***Attempted Murder:*** I recommend that a charge is raised. As per my write-up on Alex Holden, her actions during their escape from THE CreAtures showed her to attempt to sacrifice Alex. As the instigator, the charge belongs to her. Despite Sarah Walker's attempts to justify the actions, you could also make a similar case in relation to her sacrifice of Aaron Colt. I believe that a fine should be calculated and claimed via her estate.

- ***Murder:*** I recommend that a charge is raised. She killed Stuart Grant. This is irrefutable. I believe that a fine should be calculated and claimed via her estate.

File to be linked with Thornton-Hythe investigation, reference:
261426030321061922111122092607090604261022

END OF REPORT [197]

Three days ago, the police were called to a domestic incident between Josh Byrne and Alex Holden. Though the full summary of events is available upon request, it can be summarized thus:

Alex Holden returned home to find their husband Josh Byrne about to be engaged in intercourse with an ex-lover. This caused a substantial increase in Alex's stress levels, and they acted irrationally, skipping their NV. With their recognized negative emotions no longer supressed, they suffered a mass build-up of potential destructive behaviour. This manifested in them confronting Josh Byrne [several days later, the exact timeframe is uncertain] and, when he refused to talk about the incident, injecting him with their NV sample. This, they later stated, was intended to be followed by placing Josh in their assigned AS with the hope of forcing the infidelity to the surface.

Josh does not currently use the NVAS system as the medication they are using to correct several ailments—both physical and mental—are known to react badly with the standard NV components. Until he is at a point where the NVAS system can be used safely, he is among the approx. 3,000 citizens that are not part of the program. The result of using another person's NV can range from mild illness (if the dose is similar to your own) to death.

In Josh's case, Alex's NV caused him to pass out. Finding themselves unable to wake their husband, Alex panicked and subsequently began destroying the house in a rage. Hearing Alex's cries, neighbours called the police, believing there to be an intruder present. The police arrived and sedated Alex. They then summoned an ambulance and the two were taken to the local hospital for treatment.

The nature of the incident meant that it was deemed appropriate to report it to us as a Governing Body for the NVAS system. The decision was made to place both Alex and Josh in an AS to test not only the events that occurred, but the likelihood of reoccurrence.

Please note that there are no known effects relating to an AS that would negatively affect Josh. In fact, he has used basic equivalents of an AS during therapy before. It is, however, rare for a joint AS to be needed. Under the circumstances though, the results would affect both parties, so this seemed the most logical course of action.

Certain parts of the events were fed in—such as Josh sending Alex away to a Comic Con to hide his infidelity (this was factual, from what we can tell), and a slightly altered version of Alex's reaction—as this would be required to ensure accuracy in analysis.

As you can see, Josh is suffering with an extreme amount of guilt relating to his past and how it still affects him to this day. Meanwhile, Alex, too, has clearly suffered more than they have shown in public. That the AS played out the way it did does prove one thing for certain: their relationship itself is unhealthy. While neither usually commit acts that the NVAS system is designed to prevent, their interactions have exacerbated their worse traits. This, too, is the case in the AS, where their differing approach to the scenario placed before them sees a focus on said traits, despite both coming to acknowledge their mistakes.

For Josh, this meant placing himself in a living Hell; a self-imposed horror movie set in the loneliness of a cold, judgemental future where Alex was his only real bright spot. He risked losing his partner, and saw the destructive nature of his base urges and habits first-hand, in a graphic representation of self-loathing.

Meanwhile, Alex placed themselves in a position of being a pseudo judge. This was accompanied by a sense of disassociation as they applied a fictional friend to make some of the judgements, though these two almost became one and the same towards the end. As things progressed, they came to recognize that they sought to control Josh to a point, despite not truly understanding his issues. Interestingly, it was Alex's self-imposed role that causes both parties to be assuming the role of both victim and criminal in the overall story.

It is worth noting that the 'judgements' made by Alex here were mostly correct, though. While not entirely so, their interpretation is broadly similar to the analysis we undertook. The end scenario of Josh's tale would indeed have been better served with Josh's Ego and a creature surviving. If that had happened, then not only would Josh have accepted his guilt, but Alex, too, would not be at a point where they wish to walk away. This was not, however, the 'best' ending.

You see, the AS system has a built-in 'Cry for Help.' The CFH is played out by the person in the Sim submitting to the control of a governing body. This will often be portrayed as the UN, a Local Government, or the military. Unfortunately, in this instance, Josh was openly hostile towards the goals of said entities. That they appeared at all, and in a position of clear power means that part of him identified the system for what it is, but he is simply not ready to embrace it. For example, had Lucy and a creature gone to the UN rather than dying, it would mean that Josh accepted his guilt and wanted help via the NVAS system. Similarly, Alex brought in a Government contractor as a character, but chose to end the relationship rather than seek their help in fixing the underlying issues.

Had those scenarios been the endings, enforced couple's therapy may have been an option. As it is though, this appears to be a lost cause, sadly.

My recommendations relating to both parties have been accepted by the courts, and are summarized thus:

Both Josh Byrne and Alex Holden will be sentenced to mandatory therapy to help control their negative urges. For Alex, this will be via a Government-assigned therapist. For Josh, it will simply equate to a small alteration in his current therapy.

Alex Holden's NV will be reviewed with a view to potentially increasing the dosage of elements designed to decrease the need to control others.

The marriage of Josh Byrne and Alex Holden will be legally dissolved, and a new AS will be scheduled with a view to using Suggestion Technology to erase their memories of each other. This, combined with moving Josh Byrne to a neutered environment, free of temptations such as alcohol, should negate any chance of a repeat of this incident. I understand that moving Josh may seem unusual, but the fact is, he has fewer social links in the area than Alex. His removal will be far less damaging than it would be for Alex. Alex's regular contacts will be treated via their own AS to also remove the details of Alex and Josh's relationship.

If you wish to discuss the case further, please let me know. While my recommendations have been accepted, there is a forty-eight hour grace period in case you wish to bring further evidence forward in relation to either party. Otherwise, thank you for your continued use of the NVAS system and adherence to its rules and regulations.

Together, we can make the world a safer place.

ABOUT THE AUTHOR

MATT DOYLE is a pansexual/genderfluid author from the UK who primarily writes hybrid genre fiction with a sci-fi grounding and diverse characters. In recent years, Matt's work has included the award-winning LGBTQ sci-fi mystery series, THE CASSIE TAM FILES, and several anthology appearances. AILUROS is Matt's first adventure in experimental fiction.

When not working on yet another story, Matt can usually be found running the pop culture website 'Matt Doyle Media', building cosplay, and programming video games.